# Comatose

## REUBEN J PASCHAL

authorHOUSE®

*AuthorHouse*™
*1663 Liberty Drive*
*Bloomington, IN 47403*
*www.authorhouse.com*
*Phone: 1-800-839-8640*

Published by AuthorHouse   01/04/2013

ISBN: 978-1-4817-0516-5 (sc)
ISBN: 978-1-4817-0515-8 (e)

Library of Congress Control Number: 2013900298

# CHAPTER I

The clock sitting on the bedside table reads seven a.m. when the alarm shouts. A hand reaches over trying to turn it off, but has trouble finding the switch. In anger the hand picks up the clock, slinging it across the room and breaking it into a thousand pieces. The alarm shuts off for a brief second, then turns back on and then finally dies out. Sean, who is a young teenager at the age seventeen, lies in bed staring at the ceiling. He shouts with anger, "I don't want to go to School!" As he moans in disappointment, he kicks the covers off of him like a little child. He then proceeds to rise up in bed, rolling his head around and yawning as he scratches his head. He throws his legs off the side of the bed and stands up slowly. He begins walking toward the bedroom door dragging his feet along the way. As he reaches for the knob, his mother, Connie, beats him to it as she opens it quickly, knocking him in the head and to the floor. Not aware that she has done this, she looks inside with a cigarette hanging off her bottom lip and says in an angry voice, "Get your ass up!" With big blonde hair and dressed in a skimpy top, high hills, slacks and a ton of makeup on her face, she stands nervously. The half smoked cigarette bounces up and down as she speaks. The smoke burns her left eye causing her to blink uncontrollably. As she takes one long puff she asks, "What the hell is wrong with you?" Sean just lays there rubbing his head not saying a word. She walks out of the room slamming the door behind her and into the kitchen where she grabs her car keys and heads out the front door, slamming it behind her as well. She walks quickly to her car as she scrambles to find the door key. She puts the key in the car door, unlocking it and climbs inside. Slipping the key into the ignition, she tries to crank the car, but it doesn't seem to want to start. She pumps the gas pedal a couple of times and holds it to the floor. "Come on you piece of crap!" She tries cranking it one more time. "PPPOOOWWW", the car yells out as the engine backfires and then comes to a steady hum. A large cloud of smoke comes from the rear of the car filling the sky with toxic fumes. Forgetting that the driver's window is down, the smoke flows into the car making her cough her head off. She tosses her cigarette out the window, puts the car in reverse and backs out of the driveway. Then she puts the car in drive and drives off.

Sean walks out of his room fully dressed wearing saggy blues jeans, a white t-shirt and white sneakers. He walks down the hall and to his older brother's bedroom door. As he knocks twice on the door, he shouts, "Hey Adam!" but there is no answer. Sean opens the door to find Adam still lying in bed. "Get up or we'll miss the bus!" Adam pays him no mind as he rolls over moaning and groaning like an old bear. With a "Whatever" look on his face, Sean rolls his eyes and steps out of the room slamming the door behind him. Sean is constantly looking after Adam because of his mental illness. After their parents got divorced and the father disappeared, Adam became overweight and began losing his mind. He started wearing black clothing and hardly ever spoke.

Sean walks back down the hall and turns left into the kitchen. He walks over to one of the cabinets and opens a door. There is not much food in the house, because their mom spends most of her money on liquor and smokes. Sean finds a box of cereal that's probably too stale to eat and grabs the milk from the refrigerator and sets both of them on the kitchen table. He then turns around and gets a spoon from a drawer, a bowl from another cabinet and places them on the table. He pulls the chair out from the table and sits down. He opens the box and pours the cereal into the bowl. He then opens the container of milk and pours it onto the cereal. He tries to eat as fast as he can so he will not be late for the School bus. Adam walks into the room fully dressed wearing his usual black t-shirt, black jeans and black shoes with his hair dangling down in front of his face. He walks over to the cabinet and grabs a bowl from it and opens a drawer grabbing a spoon as well. He walks over to the kitchen table and sits his bowl and spoon down. At this time, Sean is about done with his breakfast as he slurps the last bit of milk out of the bowl. He gets up and throws his bowl and spoon into the sink and says to Adam, "Hurry up. We're going to be late." Adam pours the cereal and milk into the bowl and puts it up to his mouth. As big as he is it's like drinking a shot of whiskey. The cereal and milk are gone in seconds. Sean can only stand there watching him with astonishment in his eyes. Adam throws the bowl and spoon into the sink behind him and gets slowly up from his chair. "Let's go", says Sean. They both walk to the front door and out of the house. Sean is the first to walk out so he tells Adam, "make sure that door is locked". Adam locks the door and pulls it tight.

Walking down the front steps, Sean leads both of them to the bus stop, which is right around the corner. As they're approaching, Sean looks up and sees his girl friend Jessica standing with the other kids. She's wearing black jeans, a white tank top and a black bra underneath. Her hair is dyed black and blonde and tied back in a pony tail and wearing shoes that look like something that a coal miner would wear. As Sean and Adam reach the Bus stop, they are greeted by the others. Sean hugs Jessica and gives her a kiss. "I missed you", says Sean with a big smile on his face. "I missed you, too", she says. Adam, who doesn't like Jessica, stands in silence with an angry look upon his face. You could tell that he wanted to get something off his chest, but he couldn't. He wants his brother to be happy.

The School Bus rounds the corner, kicking up dust in its path as it comes to a slow stop. Slowly, the doors open and one by one the children get on the bus, impatiently shoving one another. With Jessica, Sean and Adam bringing up the rear Jessica enters first then Sean. With no problem, the two find a seat about midway and sit down. Sean looks for Adam to be right behind him, but there is no sign. He looks out the side window of the bus and sees Adam standing outside. He yells out, "Come on man. Get on the bus!" Adam proceeds as he puts one foot on the first step. He then climbs the second step as the whole bus tilts to one side. You could hear the shocks creeping as well as the kids yelling. He barely makes it through the doors, trying to catch his breath. He makes it to the top, while turning to sit in the front seat. As he passes the driver, the driver looks at him with eyes and mouth wide open. She can't believe what she has seen. As Sean looks at the back of Adams head he yells out, "you ok?" Adam doesn't reply. He just sits there trying to catch his breath. The Bus doors close and the bus drives off.

Hardly five minutes into the ride half of the kids in the back of the bus started to get rowdy as they throw balls of paper at one another, while laughing and giggling. A piece of paper hits Adam in the back of the head. He doesn't even flinch, just groans a little to himself, mumbling nastiness under his breath. A boy sitting in the back yells out, "hey freak!" Adam doesn't move a muscle. "Hey freak, I'm talking to you." He throws another ball of paper at Adam. It hits him in the head and bounces off and falls to the floor. This time the boy has pushed him too far. Adam turns around with a look of hatred in his eyes and mumbling louder. He rises out of his seat slowly with his eyes focused on the idiot that keeps bothering him. "What are you going to do about it freak?", the little boy asks with a smirk on his face. A moment of silence hits the air. Sean can do nothing but watch. Jessica reaches for Sean's hand and grips it tightly as they both look at each other knowing what is about to happen. Adam whispers, "I'll show you what I'm going to do about it". He rushes toward the back. Before the boy can speak again Adam has him by the throat, clenching harder and harder, causing the boy to have a peaked, sickly look. Adam stares him down. Tears run down the boy's face as Adam's eyebrows rise in shock, realizing what he has done. He lets go, but not before shoving the boy's head down into the seat. Adam walks back to his seat, as the rest of the children cower in silence. Wide eyed, Sean looks at Jessica and says, "What the hell, he usually beats the crap out of people like that." Adam exhausted, sits and stares out the side window wishing he could be taken away from all this. The bus driver does nothing, as if she felt sorry for Adam, maybe, because she too was picked on as a child for being different.

The bus pulls up to the School squealing brakes and pouring blue smoke from the exhaust. As the doors open everyone gets off in an orderly fashion with Adam leading the way. He waits patiently for Sean outside the bus. Sean steps off the bus and Jessica follows. As she walks by Adam, she asks with a smart mouth tone, "Why can't you be more like Sean?" Adam looks at the ground with anger in his eyes and begins to mumble. The only word she could make out was "Bitch". "What the hell did you call me?" She snaps, trying to hit him with a closed fist, but Sean steps in grabbing her arm stopping her short of just inches from Adam's face. "Just let it go!" Sean yells while staring at her in the face. She pulls her arm back and straightens her shirt. "Whatever", she says. "I've got to get to class anyway." She walks into the School as Sean follows with a mean look on his face and shaking his head. Adam, in his own little world, walks, but drags his feet to the entrance to the School.

As he walks inside, he makes his way through the packed hallway of kids. Constantly, he is bumped into by mean kids who just want the crap beat out of them. Adam just figures at this point that all he wants is to get to class especially after the incident on the bus. As he makes it to the room, there are about four kids already sat down inside. He calmly sits down in his seat specially made for him where he waits until the other students arrive. The teacher walks in with a smile upon her face and says, "Good morning Adam!" Adam, being short of words, just looks at her and smiles.

As Sean and Jessica are walking to class they run into a couple of their friends, John and Christy. "What's up?" asks John. "Hey. What's up man?" John, wearing jeans and a shirt that looks like he's been sleeping in it for a week, asks a smartass question. "Ya'll ready for another exciting day of School?" Sean replies, "HA HA NO." He rolls his eyes in boredom, trying not to say much. He just stands there trying to look cool with his girl by his side. "Hey. Jessica. Do you want to come over later and hang?" asks Christy, whom look like she could be in some dirty magazine. She dressed like Jessica with her skanky tank top, ripped jeans and pink, blonde hair. "No.", Jessica replies. "I'll probably be over Sean's house all day." "That's ok." says Christy. "Maybe we can get together this weekend." "Sounds cool", says Jessica. As the bell rings, everyone says their goodbyes and heads to class. Sean grabs Jessica's hand as they walk into their classroom.

They walk toward the back of the classroom where they take their seats. By this time, the class is filled and the teacher begins to speak. "Good morning class. Today we will be learning about a lot of things such as eating right, S.T.Ds. and above all, taking better care of you." Sean and Jessica at this point aren't paying attention at all, except to each other. The teacher yells out, "You two need to pay attention to what I am saying or leave this class." Sean and Jessica both turn away from each other as they giggle from embarrassment. "Now as I was saying, it is very important to maintain a healthy body so in doing this you need to exercise and eat properly. Do any of you know what "Diabetes" is?" The look on most of the class is confusion at this point. Sean and Jessica began to act again as if they didn't care. As the teacher explained, Sean's and Jessica's attention disorder kicked in and whatever the teacher was saying went in one ear and out the other. They didn't care to know any of that stuff. All they cared about was each other.

Back in Adam's class, the teacher brings up the subject of war. Fighting has always intrigued Adam probably because he watched his parents fight all the time when he was younger. They never cared about what he watched on TV and never taught him right from wrong. All of this added together made Adam who he is today. As he listens to the teacher, he begins to daydream, projecting himself onto the battlefield . . . "Alright men!" a General says. "I'm not going to lie to you. We're almost out of ammunition, there are only five of us left and it doesn't look like we're going home anytime soon, so let's get out there and kick some ass!" Adam picks up his riffle and begins shooting at the enemy. There's screaming and yelling all around him. One after and another, he picks the enemy off. Dramatically, the ones that are wounded fall to their knees as others lose their limbs. A soldier runs beside Adam yelling, "don't worry; I've got your back!" A bullet goes right through the man's head. The blood covers one side of Adam's face as he pauses in shock. He turns to shoot the enemy, but only gets a couple of shots off before he runs out of bullets. He slings his rifle down and pulls out his knife. He yells out, "Die!", as he holds the knife up. He doesn't take two steps when he is shot in the chest. He slowly falls to his knees. One of the enemy soldiers walks up to him and points a hand gun at his head. Adam's eyes close as a loud bang is heard. He then opens them up to find the teacher standing in front of his desk holding a ruler on one end and the other on his desk. "If you want to sleep do it somewhere else." she says. She turns and walks back up to the blackboard. Adam looks around the classroom with sweat dripping from his forehead. All of the children sit staring at him, but this is nothing new to him. Using his hand, he wipes his faces dry. He sits at his desk quietly and pretends to listen to the teacher like the rest of the class. "And that's what war is all about." says the teacher. "Are there any questions?" No one in class raises their hand. No one cares. "Come on ya'll, anybody?" the teacher asks with a disappointing look upon her face. The bell rings and the students get up and walk out of class. "We'll go over more of this tomorrow." she says. One by one the children fill the hallway, yelling and talking to one another until their next classes begin.

Adam walks down a side hall and out a set of double doors. He walks down some steps and turns to his right. "Hey, Adam!" say Sean as he leans against the brick wall of the school while smoking a cigarette. "How's your day going?" Adam shrugs his shoulders while looking at the ground. "I know what you mean man.", says Sean. Adam shares the cigarette as he takes a long puff. He blows the smoke upward and stares at the sun, letting it burn into his eyes. He closes his eyes quickly before they begin to water. Jessica appears from another side door. "Give me a drag." she says with demanding authority. Sean hands the cigarette to her while saying, "You know you could say please." She rolls her eyes, not caring what he thinks and smokes the rest of it. Adam pissed off at her already, turns and walks back into the school. As the bell rings, she throws the butt down. Sean takes her by the hand and they walk back into the school. He kisses her and says, "I'll see you after class". He turns and walks down a separate hallway. She walks the opposite way not looking back one time. He turns around, walking backwards, just to get one last look. With a smile on his face, he turns back around and keeps walking with an, "I'm the man", kind of strut until he reaches his class. As she turns a corner she stops, turns around and peeks back around to see if he's gone. He is nowhere in sight so she dashes across the hallway and runs back outside. The reasons are unknown.

"Today in Math we will be solving some different equations." says the teacher. As he reaches for the chalk, Adam pulls out a pencil and paper from his book bag. The teacher begins to write on the blackboard one of the most difficult equations anyone has ever seen. Most of the class just sits and stares, while Adam on the other hand begins copying everything the teacher writes. "Ok class. See if you can figure this one out." He lays the chalk down and walks back toward his desk. Before he can sit, Adam raises his hand. "Yes Adam", asks the teacher. "Did you have a question?" Adam slowly picks his paper up and holds it out to give to the teacher. The teacher turns and walks to Adam. The class in astonishment looks at Adam, wondering what's on the paper. He grabs the paper from Adam thinking the impossible has just happened. As he reads, his eyes grow bigger. He can't believe what he's seeing. "Where did you get this answer from?" the teacher asks with anger. The class whisper to each other. The teacher walks to the front of the classroom and makes a phone call. "Hello. Professor you know that equation you gave me to show to the class? Well one of my students I think has just figured it out. I'll read it to you." As he is doing this, Adam looks around the room as everyone stares at him. A girl catches his eye as she smiles at him. He hesitates and smiles back at her then turns his head with a shy look upon his face. The teacher hangs the phone up. He turns and walks toward Adam and says, "Congratulations. You're the smartest person I know besides my professor. So how did you know the answer?" Adam looks up at the teacher, holds up his index finger and points to his head. He then lowers his hand staring back at the teacher with a blank look on his face. "You cheated didn't you?" asks the teacher. Adam looks at him with anger in his eyebrows. "Excuse me sir", a little voice asks. "How can he be cheating when you didn't even have the answer?" "Yeah!" says the rest of the class. At this time, the teacher looks like a complete idiot. Adam looks over and sees it was the little girl that was smiling at him a few minutes ago. She looks at Adam with an, "I want you", look in her eyes. All he can do is just stare at her with a big smile. "I don't know how you did it, but I'll find out", says the teacher. He turns around and walks up to the chalkboard where he wipes away the equation quickly. He slams the eraser down and walks back over to his desk. As he sits down, he says "Ok class, time for a pop quiz!" "Ah man!" says the class.

Outside the school, Jessica leans up against the wall looking around. "Hey", a voice says. She looks to her left and it's Sean's friend John. "Hey!" she says, jumping into his arms, while wrapping her legs around his waist. She puts her arms around his neck, kissing him till the both of them let go gasping for air. "Are you coming over tonight?" he asks. "I'll be there after I go to Sean's house. I don't want him to suspect anything." "When are you going to break up with that loser?" "Just as soon as I kill him", says Jessica. "You're not really going to kill him are you?" "Yeah.", she says, with a smile on her face. "How?" he asks. "I'm going to shoot him up with a lot of cocaine when he's asleep, then I'll make sure his retarded brother has his finger prints on the syringe. Then I'll hide the syringe in Adam's room, that way when the police find it they'll think that he did it. "But why don't you just break up with him?" "Because, he'll kill me and you if I do?" "Well, in the future, if you want to break up with me just tell me. OK?" She looks at him, like the psycho she is and smiles, kisses him on the cheek and says, "See you later". She walks back into the school as John stands questioning himself.

Sean sits in his classroom listening to the teacher talk about poetry and such as he looks out the window and begins to daydream just like his brother. He imagines himself lying on his bed staring up at the ceiling when a pretty girl with long black hair and big brown eyes appears over top of him with her hair dangling down on his face. He smiles at her as she smiles back, but something is wrong. Her hair starts to fall out and her face begins to melt. Quickly, she transforms into a demon, letting out a horrible scream. Her body turns to ash and falls apart on top of him. Sean awakes screaming at the top of his lungs and sweating profusely. Everyone looks at him wondering what kind of drugs he's been taking. The teacher asks, "Are you ok Sean?" He breathes deeply and says, "Yes. I'm fine." The teacher slowly takes her eyes off of him and continues teaching. Sean, knowing he just made an ass of himself, slides down in his seat and folds his arms. He then decides for once to listen to the teacher. How many of you have ever heard of Romeo and Juliet? Now here are a couple of kids that were really in love with each other, so in love that they died for each other. They never got caught up in the superficial crap that there is today." As the teacher spoke, Sean thought about Jessica and knew his love for her was even stronger.

The last bell rings and class lets out. The School's doors open as the children begin to pour out. One by one, the children get on the School buses as they laugh and yell at one another. Sean and Jessica walk out of the School holding hands as they walk toward their bus. Jessica enters first as Sean follows her. They both find a seat about midway and sit down. Adam storms out of the School, knocking down kids as he heads toward the bus. He squeezes through the bus doors, just barely fitting and sits down in the first seat on the left. He stares out the window as it drives off. Its diesel engine clattered and raced as it hardly moved. Sean looks at Jessica and asks, "What was your day like?" She replies, "It was ok. I really don't want to talk about it, though." All she kept thinking about was John and how she was going to murder Sean. "So what do you want to do later?" he asks. "Why don't we go to the pool hall?" she asks with a devilish look in her eye. "Sounds cool, but I don't have that much money though." he says. "I want to get drunk!" she says. "I definitely don't have enough money for that." he says. "We can get drunk without money." she says. Sean looks at her with a funny face and says, "I know we can't steal my mom's alcohol. She keeps it locked up." She giggles and says, "That wasn't what I was thinking. All we have to do is go to the pool hall and look for glasses of alcohol and swipe them. It's way too busy in there for anyone to notice. No one will expect a thing." What Sean didn't know was that Jessica was planning on him being so drunk that she could get him back home in bed hoping he would pass out so she could shoot him up with drugs.

The bus arrives at the bus stop and Adam is the first to try and step off. He gets stuck so Sean has to push him from behind. "Ok. When I say go you suck in your gut." says Sean. "HA. HA." says Adam. "Ready, set, go!" Adam takes a big breath and falls off the bus with Sean landing on top of him. Jessica laughs uncontrollably as Adam yells, "Get off of me". Sean rolls off of Adam laughing as well. It takes Adam a second to get back on his feet. Jessica steps off the bus grabbing Sean's hand and walking toward their homes just up the street. As Sean and Jessica reach Sean's house they part their ways. "I'll see you in a minute." she says. "Alright", he replies. Jessica continues toward her house right beside Sean's, while Sean and Adam walk inside of theirs.

"Well, looks like we beat mom home again." says Sean. "Let's look for something to eat. I'm starving." Adam looks in the refrigerator while Sean looks in the top cabinets. "There isn't nothing in here", says Adam. "I found some doughnuts and some cookies!" say Sean. He pulls them from the cabinet and opens both packages. He grabs a doughnut and wolfs it down. Adam does the same. "Man I love doughnuts. I could eat doughnuts till I die!" says Sean. Adam just looks at him, lifting one eyebrow as he grabs the bag of cookies. As big as he is he takes a couple out at a time and puts them all in his mouth, chewing a couple of times and then swallowing. He grabs a couple more and does the same. Between the both of them, they clean the bags empty in record time. "I can't eat anymore", says Sean, while rubbing his belly up and down. "I need a tall glass of milk". His brother looks at him and starts to laugh. ""Why are you laughing?" Adam, standing beside the refrigerator, opens the door for Sean. Sean stands in front of it looking inside to find it empty. "You have got to be kidding me!" Slamming the door, he looks at Adam, who is laughing his ass off and asks, "Why are you laughing. You ate just as much as I did. Aren't you thirsty?" He stops laughing almost immediately. "You got any money?" he asks Sean. "A little, but maybe Jessica has some milk. Let's go to her house and see."

They walk outside and over to Jessica's house next door. Sean knocks on the door, but there is no answer. Just as he tries knocking again, she opens the door and says, "I was getting ready to come over." Sean replies, "I know, but we don't have any milk to drink and I was hoping that you would have some." "No. I don't have any", she says. "Well, let's just go to the pool hall", says Sean. "Ok", she says. As she walks out of her house, she closes the door behind her. Sean takes her hand, while walking beside her. Adam follows them, kicking rocks down the street with his head hanging toward the ground, while walking with a hunch. "Man, if I don't get something to drink soon I'm going to pass out", says Sean, grabbing his throat. "The pool hall is about a half a mile away. Are you sure you can make it?" asks Jessica, praying he'd die right then and there. "I'm good, just a little weak that's all", he says. As they're walking down the road cars are wising by. They find themselves entering the busiest part of town where people are working and trying to make a living. Before they reach the pool hall they come up to a corner market. A bum sitting beside the entrance asks, "You kids got any spare change?" Sean shouts, "No you freaking bum! Why don't you get a job?" The bum replies, "I can't. I'm disabled." "So why don't you get some kind of disability check?" asks Sean. "I can't!" says the bum. "The Government cut me off!" "When was this?" asks Sean. "I don't know man. Maybe it was a couple of weeks ago or maybe years ago. I can't remember. Come on man! Just give me a dollar!" Sean glances over at Adam and Jessica and whispers, "crack head." They start to walk away when Jessica stops and turns around. She walks back to the homeless man and kneels by his side. She looks into his eyes and says, "Hey mister, tell you what. I'll give you some money if you go in there and buy us some beer. "Here" She gives him a ten that she stole from her mom's purse and he takes it. "Now get us some damn beer!" she shouts. The bum hops right up and stumbles into the store. "Nicely put", says Sean. "Yeah, but let's just wait and see if he really does it or not." It's not even three minutes when the bum parades out the door holding four beers in his hand. He hands each one of them a beer as he smiles in happiness, skipping around like a little child and drinking the soulful liquid that lifts his spirits. Suddenly, he loses balance, tripping and falling face first. The bottle of beer flies from his dirty hand as he yells out, "NOOOO!" Breaking into little pieces and spilling into a puddle of suds, the bottle no longer existed. With the side of his face on the ground, he looks at the beer as it glistens in the sun on the hot pavement. Sean, Jessica and Adam can do nothing but laugh. Adam blows beer out of his nose and mouth, covering Sean's face and Jessica's shirt. "Damn it Adam!", yells Jessica. Sean wipes it from his face while saying, "gross!". The bum picks himself off of the ground and asks, "you got any more money?". "NO!" says Jessica, as she swigs the last of her beer. "But, you can have the rest of my beer", she says as she hands him an empty can. He takes it from her and turns it up, but only a drop comes out. He crushes the can and throws it on the ground. He then walks over to Sean and takes his can from him. In hopes that there is more in his can he turns it up, but it too is empty. He looks at Adam, whom is still drinking his beer and throws Sean's empty can down. His brave anticipation is about to get him in trouble as he walks up to Adam. The bum swings at Adam, missing and almost falling to the ground as Adam continues to drink. He tries a second punch, but this time Adam catches his hand with his hand. He takes the can away from his lips, squeezing the bum's hand tighter and tighter till it becomes red. "I'm sorry!" the bum shouts. He pleads, falling to the ground. "All I wanted was a beer!" Adam lets go, smacking the bum in the head with the can. He lies on the ground whimpering like a little girl as the three walk away. Adam looks back as the bum stares at him. In a way, Adam kind of felt guilty, but didn't know why. Sean reaches for Jessica and pulls her to his side as they stumble away.

"I'm still thirsty", says Sean. "We're almost to the pool hall sweetie", says Jessica. As they're both all over each other, Adam, walking behind them, shakes his head in disagreement, because he hates her so much. Instead of speaking up, he just cowards away his feelings, bottling them up and awaiting the right time to explode. "I think the pool hall is about a block away", she says. "We can walk it. No problem", says Sean, while looking back at Adam. Adam's weight problem concerns him as he begins to think about walking any further, especially after drinking that beer that left a taste of ass in his mouth. Sean looks at Adam, knowing his condition and says, "You can make it man. Come on. Pick up the pace." The sweat runs down Adam's face as he struggles to walk, waddling like a duck and breathing heavily with a high pitch sound at the end of it. "Your brother's going to have a heart attack", she says to Sean as he gets a whiff of the alcohol on her breath. He turns his head quickly to avoid it, but it's too late. "What's your problem?" she asks. "Oh nothing", he replies, as he tries to keep his face away from hers. She reaches over and grabs his face, pulling him towards her and kisses him. The look on his face is a sickly one. She pulls off as he looks at her with a fake smile, dying inside from the nasty taste and smell of ninety-eight degrees of bad breath. They continue walking until they reach their destination of fun and games. Hurting from the pain, Adam walks inside the pool hall barely fitting through the door and sits down in a chair at a table. He breaths heavily, while looking around the room to see what's going on. Sean and Jessica sit down as well, looking around the room for alcohol to steal. "I see a bottle of liquor behind the bar. Why don't you go distract the bartender while I steal It.", Sean says to Jessica. "Ok", she says. "What do I do?" asks Adam. "You just sit there and look fat." says Jessica. "Screw you!" he says. "You wish." she replies as she walks to the bar. The bottle is very easy to reach, because it sits on the end of the bar up on the shelf. "Watch my back Bro'", says Sean looking back at Adam as he walks to the bar. The pool hall at this time is packed. The bartender rushes to get drinks for everyone, not paying attention at all to what is about to go down. "Hey Bartender!" yells Jessica. He looks up from what he's doing. "Come here." she says in a flirtatious voice. He walks over as Adam sits there watching how slick she really is. "What can I get you?" the bartender asks. I just want to know one thing", she asks, while looking him up and down. "Oh yeah, what's that?" "What do you think about these?" she asks, as she pulls her shirt down to show her boobs. "What do I think about what?" he asks. Adam, drinking someone else's drink, spits it out, while laughing in the background. "My tits!" she says, as she begins to get angry. "Honey, I'm gay." he says, as he walks away. "And you need a breath mint bad!" Her mouth flies wide open as she starts to feel embarrassed. She walks back over to Adam as Sean walks up as well. "Well, did you get it?" asks Jessica. "Of course I did!" says Sean. He removes the bottle from underneath his shirt and opens it. He looks around to see if anyone is watching then takes a drink. Turning the bottle up, he swallows once then brings the bottle back down, coughing his lungs out, while leaving a bad taste in his mouth. He passes it underneath the table to avoid being caught. She looks around as well then takes a drink. She swallows about three times before letting the bottle down and coughing as well. Sean pats her on the back a couple of times. She continues coughing, while handing the bottle to Adam. He takes the bottle, shakes his head and says, "What a couple of light weights". He turns it up swallowing about five times, puts it down and burps. They look at him like he's some kind of machine. He hands the bottle back to Jessica, who's starting to feel a little tipsy and sits back in his chair and crosses his arms. "How much can your skinny ass drink?" Sean asks Jessica with a smirk upon his face. "More than you can", she says as she turns the bottle up spilling a little down her shirt.

Before they knew it, they were so drunk they couldn't see straight. Jessica was passed out on the table, while Sean was up dancing around like a maniac and having fun. Adam sits back in his chair, smoking a cigarette and feeling really relaxed. Not passing out, just feeling tired he closes his eyes and starts having thoughts of the girl from his class . . .

"Hey Adam", she says. "I've wanted you for so long.", she says, as she climbs on his desk. "I just love fat boys. Is it true what they say? The bigger they are, the bigger they are!? I want to fu . . ." Suddenly he wakes up, looking around the room, but doesn't see Sean anywhere. He looks over and see Jessica still passed out and drooling all over the table. He stumbles to his feet, pushing his way through the crowd and walking out the front entrance. He knows something's wrong, because Sean would never leave without saying something, especially if he was having a good time.

Laughing and talking to himself, Sean walks down the street not knowing of his where bouts. "Man, I've got to take a piss!" he shouts, while grabbing himself with one hand and holding the bottle of liquor in the other. He takes one last drink and slings the bottle down the road. He then finds an alley where he can possibly relieve himself from the poison that fills his bladder. "Jessica!" he says as he blinks his eyes from the salty sweat that drips from his forehead. The alcohol disorients him causing hallucinations. Shadows begin to move across the walls and sounds of evil come from rats passing by. He walks further and further into the alley until he can go no more. He leans against one of the walls and unzips his pants. Staggering, he whips it out and sprays the wall. His eyes roll into the back of his head. "Man that feels much better." As he turns to walk out of the alley he begins to feel dizzy. He grabs his head with both hands to keep it from spinning, but it only gets worse. He bends over, puking and grabbing his stomach. Only a little bit though, for most of it was fluid. He ends with dry heaves a couple of times and wipes his mouth. Just when he thought it was over he gets dizzy again. This time his heart beats fast as the sweat runs down his face. He grabs his left arm as a shock runs down it making it tense up and incapable of moving. His knees grow weak causing him to fall to the ground. Landing on his knees, his sight goes blank of details. The bright light at the end of the alley confuses him as if to think it's the way to heaven. A figure appears outside of the alley. "God?" asks Sean. The figure walks toward him asking, "Sean?" "God!" says Sean, as he falls to the hard cement, smacking his head and spraying blood. Barely keeping his eyes open, the figure approaches him. He smiles and passes out.

"Where am I?" he asks himself, while looking up at the night sky. "Man I feel great!" he says. As he walks out of the alley without a speck of dust on him, he doesn't realize that he's no longer a part of this world. He is now doing what is known as the outer body experience. His body is left lying in the alley with his head in a small pool of blood. As he walks down the street, he says to himself, "why can't I remember anything?", while scratching his head. "How did I get here?" He starts to run as fast as he can back to his house. Before he knows it, he's already in front of it, walking up to the front door. He reaches for the knob and turns it, opening the door slowly and walking in.

"Mom I'm home", he says, but there is no answer. He turns to his left and walks into the den looking around for anyone. Suddenly, he hears a snore coming from the couch. He turns to look over his left shoulder and sees his mother lying there passed out from the alcohol. "Mom I'm home. Are you ok?" At first, he doesn't know what is wrong with her until he sees the bottle of vodka on the coffee table in front of the couch. Then it hits him. He realizes his mom has a problem. He never paid attention to it before. He used to treat it like a normal thing. Now he knew it was serious. He sits down in a chair beside the couch bent over with his head in his hands. "Mom, you've got to stop drinking. It's not good for you, can't you see?" As he lifts his head from his hands, he reaches for the bottle to get rid of it, but it's too late. His mother is already cradling it in her arms, still lying on the couch curled up in a little ball. He gives up and dashes off toward his room. "If you don't want me to help you then fine, but don't expect me to help when you do.", he yells. He walks into his room and flops down on the bed, thinking about his mom's situation and not thinking about where his brother is or his girl friend. "Why didn't I notice this before?" he thinks to himself. "I've never seen her drink to the point of passing out. Maybe she's really depressed about the divorce?"

His mother stumbles past his door. Startled, Sean rises up and hops off his bed. He walks to his door slowly and pokes his head out looking left. The bathroom door slams, but doesn't shut completely. It opens slowly as Sean tip-toes to see what is going on. He hears his mom vomiting and crying at the same time. With one eye he looks around the corner and into the bathroom. He sees her lying on the floor panting for breath. "Are you ok mom?" She doesn't answer, just lies on the floor trying to catch her breath. She stumbles to her feet, grasping the counter and trying not to fall back down. As she stands, she reaches inside the medicine cabinet and pulls out a sharp razor. Standing still, Sean waits for the right moment to interject. She looks at her reflection in the mirror, crying and asking for Sean's forgiveness. "I'm sorry Sean. I should've been a better mother to you." Sean's eyes enlarge as the sharp blade touches her wrist. "No!" he yells. She looks into the cabinet mirror and sees Sean running up behind her. Because she can't believe what she is seeing, she immediately drops the blade into the sink saying, "Sean?" She looks, but there is no one there. She glances back at the blade, not believing what she almost did. With tears in his eyes, Sean looks at her asking, "Why would you do that mom?" She looks in the mirror and says, "Please God, help me". She walks by Sean and out of the bathroom. "Where are you going?" he asks. He follows her through the living room and into the kitchen. "Why won't answer me?" She grabs her car keys and walks out the front door. He follows her out and stands at the top of the steps. As she gets into her car he asks, "Where are you going?", but still she does not answer. She starts the car polluting the air with its Smokey exhaust. Sean stands helplessly, watching his mother leave him behind. As she back out of the driveway and speeds off, Sean tries running after her, but he is not quick enough. He throws his hands up in the air asking, "What the hell?" He turns around and walks over to Jessica's house next door. As he stands in front of it, he looks up at Jessica's room and sees her talking on the phone, while standing in the window. He waves his arms thinking that she sees him and then runs up to the front door. He starts to knock until he hears yelling coming from inside. He stands listening through the door, Jessica and her parents argue, but he can't quite make out what they are saying. Jessica opens the door and walks out, closing it behind her. "Sounds like your parents are on your case again, huh?" She walks past him, while reaching into her purse and pulling out her cell phone. As he walks beside her he tries to keep up. She seems to be in some kind of hurry. Looking at her he asks, "so what the hell happened last night?" She doesn't reply, just dials a number and puts the phone up to her ear. "Did I do something wrong last night?" he asks. She keeps walking as he stops and yells, "Why is everyone ignoring me? You know what, if you want to be like that fine. I don't care." He walks back to his house confused about everything. He sits down on the front steps and thinks about what happened last night, but he can only remember bits and pieces. He flashes back for a moment. "Did you get the liquor?" asks Jessica. "Of course I did." says Sean. He rubs his face with his hands, while asking himself, "Why can't I remember anything else?" He glances down at his watch as it reads seven fifty am . . . "Oh crap!" he says, jumping up and running to the bus stop as fast as he can. He rounds the corner to see Jessica and Adam standing with the other kids patiently waiting to go to School. As she rambles on the phone, Adam stands quietly looking at the ground. "Hey guys." says Sean. He walks up to Adam and asks, "Hey man, what happened last night? Last thing I remember is taking a couple of shots of liquor. They funny thing is I woke up in an alleyway. That's the last time I go drinking with you guys. By the way, did you know mom was passed out on the couch when I got home?" Adam doesn't answer. "Dude, you hear me?" Adam looks up and whispers, "Something bad happened." "What are you talking about? What happened?" Jessica pulls the phone away from her ear and asks Adam, "What did you say?" He looks downward, but doesn't say anything. Rolling her eyes, she puts the phone back up to her ear and keeps on talking. "Who's she talking to?" asks Sean, while pointing to her. He can't quite make out the words, but it sounds like she's talking about her clothes. "What's the big deal? She's just talking about girl stuff", he says.

The School Bus appears around the corner. Its hot brakes squeal as it comes to a halt. The diesel smell nauseates the children, coughing and gagging. With Adam bringing up the rear, one by one the children load up the bus anxiously. The bus tilts as Adam struggles to climb the steps barely fitting through the doors. His breathing intensifies as his shirt soaks itself in sweat. "You going to make it son?" the driver asks. Adam grunts as he reaches the top feeling like he accomplished something greet. As he walks by the driver, the fried chicken smell of salty sweat overwhelms him. Like mustard gas the stench engulfs the bus as children cry out, "ewe! Gross!" while trying to hold their noses. Adam squeezes himself into the seat on his left, taking up the whole thing. Jessica sits about halfway up in a seat by herself, while still talking on the phone. Sean sits down in a seat in front of her, wondering who she keeps talking to. Frustrated with the lack of communication, he shakes his head and turns back around in his seat. He looks out the window with anger and sadness. She giggles behind him with the phone up to her ear, flipping her hair around and smiling contently. Adam, with somewhat of a disadvantage, turns his head around to look at Sean. A strange glow surrounds Sean's head. Adam doesn't believe what he's seeing. He turns back around and looks out of his window.

As the Bus arrives at School, it pulls into a lot filled with other buses. The children step out of their buses and walk to their classes. Adam is last to get off, pouring his overweight body onto the ground. He pauses to collect himself, gasping for air and wipping the sweat from his forehead. As he looks to his right, he sees Jessica talking on her cell and giggling. Sean stands beside her trying to communicate and waving his arms up and down. He gives up and walks over to Adam asking, "so you going to ignore me now?" "No.", says Adam. He tries not to make eye contact. "Why is everyone ignoring me?" asks Sean. "That night at the pool hall, well, you drank a little too much. You disappeared so I had to go looking for you. I found you in an alley. You had some kind of seizure or something. You hit your head and there was so much blood. I didn't know what to do. I ran back to the pool hall to get help. The ambulance came." Sean looks at Adam thinking, "what a moron." "What you think I'd make this up?" asks Adam. "Dude, you really are screwed up. Not only don't I believe you, but look at my head! No gash!" says Sean, pointing to his head. Adam gets angry and says, "You think I'm messing with you?" Sean looks at him as if to say yes. "Well screw you then. Adam storms off tugging at his shirt and pants. In total denial, Sean stands shaking his head thinking his brother has finally lost it.

The bell rings and Sean follows Adam into the School. The hallways are empty at this time as Sean yells out, "I'll see you after class." Adam turns around to say something to him, but there is no one there. Sean turns around and walks the other direction. As he walks by a room he catches a glimpse of Jessica sitting in the back. The teacher is talking to the class face to face until she turns around to write on the blackboard. Jessica takes the opportunity to lean over and give the boy sitting beside her a kiss. All Sean can see is the back of her head and can't quite make out who the guy is. In a rage, he hit the closed door, interrupting the class and causing Jessica to pull away from the guy she's kissing, exposing his face. Sean, sickened with astonishment, can't believe his own eyes. "John?" he says to himself. The teacher walks over to the door to see who is there. "Crap!" he says. He darts away quickly thinking the teacher might see him. Of course, the teacher examines the hallway only to find it bare. Sean stops a couple of lockers down, waiting patiently for Jessica's class to be over. As time goes by, Sean sits on the floor wondering what he's going to say. Finally the bell rings, letting the classes out. Sean stands and waits for Jessica to walk out with John. As they exit, they stop and kiss one another as this only throws gasoline on the fire. "I'll see you later", says John, as he turns and walks away. She smiles then turns toward Sean, flicking her hair as she walks by him. "How could you do this to me after all we've been through? I trusted you." says Sean. "What? Are you not going to say anything you heartless bitch?" She walks to her locker and opens it. "I see you still have pictures of me in your locker." She glances at the pictures with a sigh and rips them down. "What the hell?" he asks. She slams the locker shut and turns to walk off. He tries to grab her arm, but his hand goes right through it. It startles him, making his pulse race. Just to check for his sanity, he sees a guy walking by and tries to grab him with both hands, but ends up falling down. He sees a crowd of people walking his way, but is unable to get out of the way. He covers his face in protection as the crowd walks over him, but leaves him untouched and unharmed. He scrambles to his feet, checking himself for damage only to find that there is nothing wrong. "They didn't touch me. They went right through me.", he says. Then there's a distraction coming from around the corner. "Now what?" he asks, while walking to see what all the commotion is about.

He turns the corner and sees three guys jumping his brother, two holding him, while the third punches. Adam falls to his knees as he coughs in agony. Sean rushes through the crowd without touching a single person. He tries to grab the guy punching Adam, but falls right through him. Somehow, Adam finds the strength to wrestle himself away from one of the guys and punches him in the groin. Still on his knees, Adam then pulls the other guy's feet out from under him causing him to fall backwards, hitting his head on the concrete floor. It knocks him out cold. As for third guy trying to hit him, he catches his fist, bringing him down to eye level. "AH!" the guy cries out as Adam breaks every bone on his hand. The other kids chant, "Fight, fight, fight". Sean can only sit back and watch as Adam looks at him and smiles, while sitting on one of the guy's face. He then lets out the most God awful sound, breaking wind and saying, "now that's the advantage of being fat!" while looking down at the guy. Adam rolls off the guy and slowly rises to his feet. About dead from the lack of air, the guy coughs as he sets up, stands and runs off. Sean walks over to Adam and starts to ask, "Are you ok?", when a girl walks up to him instead and asks the same thing. Adam recognizes her as the girl he likes from his class. "Yeah, I'm ok." He says. "My name is Amber", she says with a smile. "Don't you have a name?" He pauses. "Adam," "Well Adam, why did those guys jump you?" Adam looks at her with a gleam in his eye and asks, "How did you know I didn't jump them?" Sean laughs in the back ground. "I see", she says. "Well, I've got to get back to class. Maybe I'll see you around." Adam looks at her and smiles, "maybe", he says. As she walks one way he walks another, while looking back and smiling. Sean looks at him, but doesn't say a word, just shakes his head as Adam walks by.

After the hallway is cleared Sean is left standing alone looking around and wondering where to go. He walks a little ways down the hall when he stops to look at weird shadows on the walls. He begins hearing strange voices coming from behind. He turns around, but finds no one standing there. "Hello!" he shouts. He turns back around and keeps on walking. "Sssseeeeaaaannnn", a voice whispers. He becomes angry and yells, "what?" He turns back around to see the Grim Reaper standing at the other end of the hall, reaching out with its boney hand, dressed in a long black gown, ripped and waving in the wind. It holds in its other hand a six foot tall scythe with a three foot blade and a gruesome look that would make any man beg for mercy. The Reaper has no face, just a black hole in time and no patience for anyone. Sean, too scared to move, closes his eyes and listens to the breath of the Reaper as it gets closer and closer. "Just run", he tells himself. He turns around with his back toward the Reaper and takes off, leaving the Reaper standing still. It reaches out for Sean, letting out a horrible roar, but Sean is too fast for it. He runs down the halls, rounding corner after corner. He finally finds the front door of the School, exiting it as fast as he can. He is met with a blinding white light, causing him to blackout and reawaken in his bed.

"It was all a dream", he says to himself. He hops out of his bed with a smile upon his face, walks out of his bedroom and into the kitchen. He stumbles upon his mother, who looks terrific and his brother neatly dressed with a haircut, both sitting at the dinner table accompanied by two small children, about the ages of five and six and a man in his forties. "Hey mom!" says Sean. "What's going on?" She doesn't reply, but instead keeps eating. He pauses and looks at his brother and asks, "what happened to you?" Adam doesn't reply as well, just keeps eating. "Who are these people mom?" asks Sean, as he points to them, but still there is complete silence. The man, grabbing his napkin to wipe his mouth, says, "This is the best steak I've ever had." "Thank you", she says with a grin. "I haven't had a chance to make a meal like this in a long time." "Well, it's delicious", he exclaims. "Yeah, it's good mom." Says Adam. "Mom are you going to see Sean tonight?" he asks. "Why? Do you want to see him?" "Yeah", he says. Sean looks at both of them with big eyes and asks, "What are ya'll talking about? I'm right here", he says, pointing at himself. "Has everyone gone crazy? Why won't you answer me?" Sean begins to panic having shortness of breath and dizziness. He falls to the floor and blacks out.

Sean awakens to find himself under water, alert and trying to reach the top. Climbing his way upward he bumps his head into a thick sheet of ice. He hits it hard, backing off and grabbing the top of his head. The pain only angers him as he tries breaking through the ice with his fist. A girl from above about the same age as Sean wearing thick clothes, a toboggan and gloves, looks downward and sees Sean begging for his life. She stares for a moment in shock. "Mom!" she yells, as her mom rushes over, trying not to slip on the ice. She gets to her and asks, "What is it honey?" The frantic girl responds with, "There's a boy stuck underneath the ice!", while pointing down. With a not believing look upon her face, her mom looks down and asks, "Are you sure honey? I don't see anyone." She looks back and forth just to make sure. "Don't you see him?" the girl asks with a cry in her voice pointing straight to him. "He's right there!" Sean beats on the ice, not believing that he hasn't run out of air by now. The girl runs off the ice and into the woods. "Where are you going?" her mom asks. "Honey there's nothing there." she says motioning toward the ground. She looks back down hearing a thump. At first, she thinks her mind is playing tricks on her. The thump continues as she covers her mouth and cries, "Oh my God!" The girl reappears from the woods running, while carrying a large branch in both hands. With each breath, the steam pours from her mouth. As she reaches him, she says to her mother, "Get out of the way!" Her mother backs up as she whacks the ice, breaking it through. It was just enough to let Sean stick his head out and catch his breath. "Help me!" Sean yells. The mother stares at her daughter wondering what kind of medication she going to get her. "Honey, I heard a thump, but there's no one there." She stands watching her daughter reaching into the water, panicking and trying to save Sean's life. Reaching down, the mother grabs the girl's arm. "Let go of me!" she shouts. She shoves her mother back making her fall to the ground. The girl franticly peels away the ice, freeing Sean from the clutches of Hypothermia and pulling him up onto the top. She holds him in her arms as he shutters from the cold. "You're ok. Shhhh." she whispers. As she looks back at her mother, she tells her, "He's ok." smiling and not realizing that no one else can see him. "Someone get some help!" As she turns back to look at Sean, she notices that she is looking at nothing, but ice. Sean had vanished into thin air. "Where did he go?" she asks. With a confused look on her face, she looks back into the water thinking that he might of slipped back in, but he was nowhere to be found. Her mom walks over putting her arms around her and says, "Let's go honey." As the tears swell up in her eyes, the girl motions toward the icy water and says, "But he was right here." Her mother can do nothing, but tell her, "I know honey. I know."

Sean ends up back in the water sinking deeper into the clutches of the freezing liquid of death. The water grabs his body like a cactus pricking every inch of his skin causing excruciating pain then leaving him numb from head to toe. The water turns black within an instant till Sean is seen no more. Silence fills his ears as he becomes disoriented and faint. "Where am I?" he thinks to himself. "Am I dead now? I can't feel the water around me. I can't feel any more pain." He lies in a vast emptiness of space with nothing around him, nothing, but darkness. Suddenly, a roar of terror erupts from underneath him. He looks downward as a bright light shines upon his face. As the light blinds, he tries to cover it with his hand, but cannot. He squints as he sees a figure approaching him getting closer and closer. Frightened, he tries to move, but cannot. "Sean", a voice whispers. "Sean". As he opens his eyes, a beautiful young woman floats in front of him dressed in white rags from head to toe with long blonde hair and perfect skin. He looks at her and smiles feeling relaxed and without fear. She smiles back letting him know everything's ok until the light bellow them begins to fade as well as her looks. His smile turns to a frown as he watches her turn from young to old in a matter of seconds. She looks down at her hands whimpering in sorrow. Looking back up at Sean, a fierce roar comes from the old woman as her mouth opens exposing large pointy teeth and a serpent like tongue. Sean struggles to turn around as if to run away, but can't. She grabs him with snake like tentacles rapping around him and squeezing every last breath out of him. He tries to escape, but more tentacles cover his body keeping him in her clutches. "Is this the end?" he asks himself. "I don't want to die!" he tries yelling. "I don't want to die . . . ."

Sean awakens from underneath a blanket wrapped tightly around his body, so tight he can barely get loose. Sweating profusely, he unravels himself and throws the covers off the bed freeing his mind from what has just happened. A girl stands at the foot of the bed combing her hair, while staring at herself in the mirror. "Hey", he says, but she doesn't answer. "Where am I?" he asks. Still, she doesn't answer. For a split second he thinks, "I might be dead." He lies still and watches her groom herself with a smirk upon his face. "Knock. Knock." ""Come in!" she says. As the door opens, Sean can't believe his eyes. "Jessica?" "Hey. Patricia. How are you doing?" "Good. I'm getting ready to go out." "Oh. Ok. Well, the reason I stopped by is because I wanted to see if you wanted to catch a movie, but since you're going out maybe later." "By the way, says Patricia, I'm sorry to hear about your boy friend." "I'm not. I hope he dies." "Whoa! Why do you want him to die?" asks Patricia. "I was only going out with him, because I was using him. I thought he was the one until I met John. Now there's a man with everything. His parents are so rich and one day it will be all his. "So what does your ex look like? Maybe I'll go out with him." "Be my guest." "In fact, go see him in the hospital. There's no telling when he'll come out of his coma." "Yeah, I might do that." "Well, anyway, I guess I'll see you later." "Ok. See you." Jessica leaves as Sean sits up on the bed looking at the girl. He suddenly recognizes her. "You're the girl that pulled me out of the ice." She puts her hair brush down and walks out of her room. "Damn you Jessica. After all this time it was a lie." Sean thinks to himself. "And when the hell did I end up in the hospital?"

He walks out of the room and down some stairs that lead him to the den. He looks and sees the girl's mom whom he recognizes from the lake. She is sitting on the couch watching TV and snacking on a bowl of popcorn. "Hurry up honey! It's about to start!" she yells. A man walks in with a drink in each hand and hands her one of them. He sits down and puts his arm around her as they begin to watch a movie. Patricia walks out from the kitchen behind Sean saying, "See ya'll later!" "Have a good time honey!" her mom says. "Be back by eleven ok." says her dad. "OK.", she replies, as she exits the house, closing the door behind her. Sean decides to follow her by walking up to the closed door. He tries grabbing the knob, but his hand slips right through it. "You've got to be kidding me!" he says. He closes his eyes and walks through the door slowly.

Instead of ending up on the front steps, he is thrown into a room filled with people he does not know. They are all sitting in chairs formed in a circle, each person with name tags on their chests. A door opens behind him. He turns around and is met face to face with his mother. She walks right through him leaving him with a shocked look on his face. "Sorry I'm late", she says. Sean reads on the door as it closes, "Alcoholics Anonymous". He turns back around and looks at his mom. He smiles, because he is glad to see her here. "I'd like to welcome everyone for coming", a lady says. "We all know why we're here so let's get started with this young lady sitting next to Me.", she says, while looking at Sean's mom. His mom stands up and begins introducing herself. "Hello, my name is Connie and I'm an alcoholic." "Hi, Connie", says everyone. She catches the eye of a man, the same man that was at her dinner table earlier. Sean recognizes him as well as he walks over to his mother. Smiling, he kneels down between her and the councilor and listens to the other people introduce themselves. "I'm glad that you're doing this mom", he says with tears in his eyes. "I want you to know that I love you very much." "Run.", she whispers. "What?" he asks. "Run!" she yells. He rises to his feet and looks at the councilor. The councilor stands holds the giant "Scythe" and pointing at him. The councilor morphs into the Grim Reaper. "Sssseeeeaaaannnnn." it says with a roar. Sean turns to run from it, but can't. The Reaper grabs him from behind with its huge hand gripping around Sean's waist. He struggles to get away, but can't. It pulls Sean toward him making him weak, squeezing tighter and tighter. He looks at his mother as he watches a tear run down her cheek. "Ha Ha Ha", the Reaper laughs. This only makes Sean mad. He grabs the Reaper's rotten ringers with both hands and pulls them apart, snapping them into. The Reaper drops him as he yells. "Ahhhh!" Sean crawls on the floor, darting toward the door. He dives through it with the Reaper right on his heels. Instead of landing on the floor on the other side, Sean continuously falls through white clouds as if he were almost flying. The clouds slowly disappear as he falls helplessly. He begins to yell, "Ahhh". He falls about a thousand feet before crashing through a hospital roof and onto a bed. "Uhh", he says.

"Sean? Sean? Can you hear me? I think he's coming out! Someone get the doctor!" says a woman's voice. A doctor rushes into the room and stands over him pointing a light into Sean's eyes. "Can you hear me Sean?" he asks. He moans a little. "Mmm, mom?" "I'm right here Sean." she says, crying with a smile. He looks to the left side of the bed and sees an old familiar face. "Dad" His dad grabs his hand and smiles. "Where am I?" Sean asks. His dad replies, "You're in the hospital. You were in a coma." His dad looks at his mom and then back at him and says, "For about a half a year." Sean pauses and asks, "What happened?" His mom explains to him. "You had what is called a "Diabetic episode". The doctor can explain it better than I can." The doctor interjects and says, "Sean, the best way I can explain it to you is that your blood sugar got too high, which caused you to be disoriented and maybe feel even drunk. Plus the amount of alcohol we found in your blood stream didn't help either as well as you hitting your head. You're real lucky you didn't die. You have your brother Adam to thank for that. If he hadn't called nine one one when he did then we probably wouldn't be talking right now. Anyway, do yourself a favor and take it easy for a while. We still want to run some test just to make sure you're ok." The Doctor turns around to leave the room, but not before saying, "by the way, your heads going to hurt for a little while so I'll bring you something." Sean smiles and says, "Thanks Doc." "Sean.", his mom says. "There's someone here to see you. Apparently, she knows you." She walks in the room and smiles. "Hello Sean. Do you remember me?" He looks at her and says with a smile, "yes I do". "How are you feeling?" she asks. "Ok, I guess." he replies. "So how do you two know each other?" his mother asks. "Well . . ." Sean begins to say until Patricia says, "We know each other from School." "Oh, ok." says his mother. Sean and Patricia make eye contact with the same thing running through their minds. "So, are you and Dad back together Mom?" asks Sean. "No son", she replies, "but we are on better terms now." she says while looking at his father and smiling. "I notified your father as soon as you had your accident." "Where have you been all this time Dad?" "I've been living in Hawaii with my soon to be wife. Maybe you can come stay with us for awhile if you like and if it's ok with your mother." "Yeah, that would be cool." says Sean. "I've really missed you Dad. I thought I'd never see you again." "Don't worry son. Everything is going to be ok." says his father. "Can you and Mom excuse me and Patricia for a moment?" "Sure son." says his mom. His parents walk out of the room

27

leaving Patricia behind. She walks over to his bed and sits on the side of it. "Do you believe in Guardian Angels?" she asks as she smiles. "Maybe.", he says. "I don't think that we know we are, but some of us have an idea." she says. "That day at the lake . . . my mom couldn't see you, in fact no one could, no one but me. Why is that?" "I don't know", he says. "And how did you get out of the ice after you vanished from my arms?" she asks. "When I asked your parents what had happened they said that you hit your head and went into a coma. Was this when you got out of the ice?" Apparently, she didn't know the truth. Sean had to explain to her what he remembered. When he told her she couldn't believe what she was hearing. "Wait, so you're telling me that you were doing some kind of outer body thing when I pulled you out of the ice? My parents thought I was crazy, but I knew I wasn't.", she says. "This is too much to process", she says, as she walks over to a chair and sits. "Maybe you are my Angel." he says. She looks at him and smiles. "That's a pretty big responsibility. I'll just have to hang around you a lot more now." she says with a smile. He smiles back. "So how did you know that I was here" asks Sean. "Jessica told me. I didn't know that was you in the lake until I came to see you here about six months ago. In fact, I've been here almost every day." "Why did you keep coming back?" "I think there might be something between us." Sean thinks to himself, "I hope so."

After a couple of days, Sean is released from the hospital. "Are you ready to go Sean?" Patricia asks, as she rolls a wheelchair into the room. "Yup.", he says, as he puts his shirt on. His mom and dad walk in behind Patricia. "Hello son. How are you feeling?" his dad asks. "I feel great!" His mother walks over to him and kisses him on the cheek. "Well, what are we waiting for?" asks Sean. He hops into the wheelchair and takes off. "Wait Sean!" his family says.

All of them exit the hospital when Sean asks, "Where is Adam?" A car pulls up in front of them as it screeches its tires to a halt. The driver exits the car. It's Adam. "What's up Bro?" "Adam?" asks Sean, as he stares with surprise. "Adam runs around the car to hug his brother. "I hardly recognized you bro. How'd you lose so much weight?" asks Sean. "When you went into the hospital I decided to turn my life around. I was tired of everyone picking on me so I started working out. I also met a girl so you know." They both smile and laugh together. "Anyway, let's get you home, man." Sean climbs out of the chair and into the car. His dad walks over to Adam and says, "Go easy on my car ok." "Sorry dad." he says with a smile. The whole family, including Patricia, get into the car and head toward the house. "Is everyone buckled?" asks Adam. "Yes", says everyone. Adam puts the car in drive and takes off. He races out of the parking lot and onto the main road. "You drive like a maniac son", says his mother. "I agree", says his father. "Slow down!" Sean tries to catch himself from falling all over the place. "Why are you in such a hurry Adam?" asks Sean. "I got a pain!" he says as he grips the steering wheel. His face turns red. "Are you ok son?" his dad asks.

The car pulls into the driveway. Everyone except Sean's father gets out of the car. Adam runs while everyone else walks into the house. His dad slides over from the passenger seat to the driver's. Sean leans in the window of the car and hugs his dad. "I'll be back in the morning to pick you up." "Ok Dad." Sean turns and walks to the front door where Patricia waits for him. They walk inside, closing the door behind them.

"Are ya'll hungry?" his mother asks. I'm not." says Sean. "No thank you." says Patricia. "What about you Adam? Are you hungry after that episode you just had?" He looks at her and asks, "Depends on what you're making." "How 'bout a sandwich?" she asks. "Sounds good." he replies. Sean pays them no mind as he walks into his room.

He sits down on his bed and begins to take his shoes off. As he does, Patricia walks in. "Here, let me help you with that." She kneels down and takes off his shoes. "Thanks.", he says. She stands back up and sits down beside him. "You know you don't have to take care of me.", he says. "I know, but I want to." He's not used to a girl treating him nice. She leans over and kisses him. "I like you Sean. I like you a lot." "I like you, too." About an hour goes by as they lay on the bed making out. Adam comes knocking on the door. "Knock knock!" Without Sean saying come in, Adam barges in and asks while eating an apple, "whatcha doing?" Sean is sitting on the side of the bed beside Patricia. "Nothing." they say. "Why are you both all red?

Were you two just getting it on?" "Dude!" says Sean. "It's ok Sean." says Patricia. "Yes Adam. I like your brother very much and yes we were trying to get it on until you came in.", she says with a sarcastic smile. Adam smiles and says, "Sorry." and exits the room.

Later that night, Patricia walks out the front door. "I guess I'll see you later." says Sean as he kisses her goodbye. She walks down the front steps as he closes the door.

He walks back into his room. "Knock knock." "Come in." "Hey man. Did you bang her?" asks Adam. Sean just smiles as he lies on his bed watching TV . . . "I'm just messing with you dude. She seems like a nice girl." "Yeah, she is." "Look, there's something I've been meaning to tell you." Sean turns his TV off. "What is it?" "A lot of stuff has been going on since you've been in your coma." "Like what?" "Mom started going to "A.A." meetings. She quit smoking. That's why she looks a lot better. She also met a man in there and we're going to be moving in with him soon. I even think mom's going to marry him. There's something else that I didn't want to tell you, but you need to know. Jessica has been cheating on you. I've known this for a long time, but never had the guts to tell you. She's with John now. I saw them making out at School, but they didn't know that I knew." Sean pretended not to know about it. "That bitch!" he says. "But you got Patricia now so everything is ok, right?" Adam was concerned that his brother would have a mental break down. "Patricia is really cool and a whole lot better looking than Jessica anyway." Says Adam. "Yeah she is", says Sean. "Well, I thought I'd tell you. I'll leave you alone." "Hey, are you coming to Dad's with me?" asks Sean. "No. I'm staying here with mom. Get some rest. I'll see you in the morning." "Hey Adam, thanks for everything." "No problem. Night." "Night."

The next day, Sean awakens. He gets up out of bed and puts on his clothes. He walks out of his room and into the kitchen. His mom stands cooking breakfast. His brother sits at the table waiting to be served. "Morning sweetie. Did you sleep ok?" asks his mother. "Yeah.", he replies, rubbing his eyes. "Have a seat dude. Mom's cooking up some good stuff." says Adam. "I bet you're starving, huh?" asks his mother. "Yeah." "Your Dad will be here shortly. So don't waste time."

She hands him a plate filled with bacon, eggs and toast. "This looks really good Mom. Thanks." says Sean. "You're welcome, sweetie."

Sean walks out of his house with his book bag and suitcase filled with clothes. He sets them down and sits on the top step. As he waits for his Dad to pick him up, a gust of wind blows. He looks over to his left and sees the "Grim Reaper" standing in front of Jessica's house. Sean frightened, doesn't move a muscle fore he fears that the Reaper might see him. As the Reaper walks by flowers, they turn black and wilt. He floats fast across the lawn and through the front door of Jessica's house. Sean's father pulls up in his car and beeps the horn. Sean grabs his book bag and suitcase quickly as he runs to the car. He opens the door as fast as he can and hops in. "Can't wait to get to Hawaii, huh?" his Dad asks. The car drives off. Sean, sitting in the back seat, turns around and looks out the back window as to think the Reaper is following him. He sees nothing and turns back around. Suddenly, there is a roar and a scream. He looks back and sees Jessica running out of her house. The Reaper follows her and grabs her by the leg holding her upside down as she squirms. "Let me go!" she yells. The Reaper takes his scythe and cuts her legs off in one slice. As he holds her legs, the upper half of her torso flops around on the ground pouring blood and guts. The Reaper looks over to Sean quickly and drops her legs. He points at him as if to say, "I'll be back for you". It, along with Jessica's torso and legs, vanish into thin air. Sean turns back around in his seat. "What's the matter? You look like you've seen a ghost." his Dad asks. Sean kind of looks to the side and says, "I'm ok."

The police and ambulance pull up to Jessica's house from the other direction. Jessica's mother runs out of the house screaming, "My baby!" while her father stands on the front steps. The police try calming her down, but it is no use. The paramedics enter Jessica's room to find her lying on her bed with a needle sticking out of her arm. "Looks to me like she died of an apparent overdose", says one of the paramedics. Her body is brought out of the house on a stretcher and in a body bag. Her mother stands and watches helplessly as the officers ask her and her husband questions.

The next day, Sean answers his cell phone. "Hello". "Hey, it's Patricia! I can't wait till you get back so we can spend more time together. By the way, did you hear what happened to Jessica? It's a shame isn't it? I mean, who knew she wanted to kill herself. At least, that's what everyone thinks. See, she used to be my best friend until she started sleeping with my boy friend. That's right. I used to date John until I found out he was sleeping with her. It was only a matter of time till I got my revenge. When I left your house last night I didn't go straight home. I went over to her house while she was all alone. She invited me in. We went up stares to do some drugs that John had given her. She took out a syringe, filled it up and put just enough in her arm to knock her out. Once she was out I took the opportunity to give her the whole thing. Wasn't my fault she couldn't handle her drugs. The best thing is when they find the finger prints on the syringe the only ones they will find are Jessica's and John's. I hope that you're happy that I did this. I did this for us. Oh and if you're thinking of leaving me think twice. "Click".

# CHAPTER 11

S ean is staying with his dad in Hawaii where he recovers from his coma. They live in a two bedroom house in a small village near the ocean and his dad owns his own scooter shop.

Sean, holding the phone to his ear, can't believe what he has just heard. He slowly brings the phone down from his ear and stands with his mouth wide open. At a loss of words, he throws the phone across the room and stands mad and confused. His dad walks in the front door and closes it behind him. He looks to the right and sees the broken cell phone on the ground. "What the hell happened here?", he asks. He looks over to Sean and stares at him. Sean doesn't say a word. He just stands there with a red face and tears in his eyes. "Who was that on the phone Sean?" Sean replies, "wrong number". "Why are you so upset then?" "I just don't feel very well right now." "Maybe you should go lay down son." Sean doesn't say a word, just walks to his room and slams the door. His dad walks over to what's left of the phone and picks up the pieces. Amazingly, it turns on. He checks the last call and sees it's Patricia. Walking over to the garbage can, he throws it away. He then walks down the hall to Sean's room and knocks on the door. "Yeah"? "Can I come in?" "I guess." His dad opens the door, walks in and stands in the doorway. "Are you ok son?" "My head just hurts. That's all. I just need to lay down." "So what's up between you and Patricia? It's ok. You can be straight with me." "One minute everything's going great, the next, it's

33

going down the toilet." "Woman can be cruel sometimes, just look at me and your mother. Hell, I had to move to another state." "What happened to you and mom anyway?" "We just couldn't get along anymore. Some people just grow apart. We tried our best." "Well, you should've tried harder." His dad turns to leave the room, but not before saying, "Get some rest. We have a big day tomorrow." "What are we doing?", asks Sean. His dad stops and turns his head to say, "I'm gonna teach you how to shoot a gun." He proceeds to leave the room shutting the door behind him.

The next day, Sean awakens to the sounds of a bird chirping outside his window. "Shut up damn bird!" He tries to roll over and go back to sleep, but it's no use. He throws the covers off of him and hops out of bed. He walks over to his closet and pulls out a shirt and jeans. He puts them on and walks out of the bedroom without putting his shoes on. As he walks down the hall and into the kitchen he is greeted by his dad standing in the kitchen. "Morning. I hope you are hungry. I made you some breakfast." "Yeah. I could eat.", says Sean, while rubbing his eyes. He pulls a chair out from under the kitchen table and sits down. His dad takes a frying pan from the stove filled with eggs and bacon and serves it on a plate sitting in front of Sean. "Eat up son. You're gonna need your energy." "So, you're gonna teach me how to shoot, huh?" "That's right. We're going to the gun range and fire off some rounds with my fourty-five." "That sounds like fun." "Have you ever fired a gun before Sean?" "No. Of course not. Why do you have a gun anyway?" "Well, I got mugged a while back and ever sense then I've felt I've needed to have one." "So . . . . Do you have it on you now?" His dad pulls the side of his shirt up exposing the gun's handle and smiles. Sean smiles a little with concern. "Cool.", he says, as he stuffs his face.

Sean exits the house first, as his dad follows, shutting the door behind him. They walk to his dads car, but just before they get in, his dad says catch, as he throws Sean the keys. When Sean catches them he asks, "what are you doing? You know I don't have a license." His dad replies, "You know how to drive don't you?" "I guess." "Then drive." His dad walks to the passenger side, opens the door, gets in and shuts the door. Sean doesn't argue. He opens the driver's door and get in. As he shuts the door, he puts the key in the ignition and starts it up. "Maybe one day this car will be yours.", his dad says with a smile. Sean smiles back and says, "I sure hope so." He shifts the car into reverse and backs out of the driveway. oy then shifts it into drive and proceeds down the road. As Sean drives, he begins to daydream about all that has been happening to him. He thinks of Jessica and how the Reaper took her away, chasing her out the front door of her house and cutting her in half. It startles him for a brief second making him run off the road. "Damn boy! Watch where you're going!", his dad yells. "Sorry. Thought I was going to hit a squirrel." "Just stay on the road. That's all I ask." His dad takes a deep breath. Sean tries to concentrate on driving, as he comes to a stop at a stop light. He yawns and stretches his arms, while looking to his left. As he looks at the car stopped beside him on his left, the Grim Reaper sits in the passenger seat looking forward with its sythe hanging out the window. Sean pretends not to see him, but looks over at him anyway, but when he looks back there is no one there except some old man driving the car. Sweet roles down Sean's face as the light turns green. Sean floors it, burning the tire up. "Slow down Sean." He backs off a little bit, but not before his dad can say, "You're gonna miss the turn." Sean turns the wheel so sharp the car almost flips over. As it straightens, his dad yells, "pull over." Sean quickly pulls to the side of the road and puts the car in park. "Get out!", his dad says. Both of them exit the vehicle as his dad walks over to the driver's side. "My turn to drive.", he says. Sean doesn't say a word. With his head hung in shame, he walks to the passenger side and gets in. His dad gets in as well.

They arrive at the gun range a bit later. They both exit the car and walk inside of the building. There they are greeted by a creepy old man missing one eye, one arm and one leg. Sean can't help, but stare at him. "Well, what do ya'll want?", he asks. "My son and I would like to shoot a couple of rounds." "Ok. Come on in." The old man stands behind a counter as Sean and his dad walk into the other room. His dad knows the place really well so he knows what to do. "Come this way Sean. Stand here and I will set up the target for you. Here, put these ear pertectors and glasses on." Sean grabs them and puts them on. "Here's my gun.", his dad says, as he pulls it out of his waist. "The safety is off. Just pull the triger back. Now you're ready to shoot." Sean becomes nervous as he points the gun at the target. "Now when you're ready just squeeze the triger." Just as his dad says this, Sean fires off a round. "POW". He barely hits the target. He fires again and again. Each time he shoot he gets closer and closer to the target. Before he knows it, he is out of bullets. "Not bad son. Not bad at all." His dad looks at him and smiles. "Now it's my turn." Sean hands him the gun. He takes the clip out and puts a new one in. He pulls the top back and points the gun at the target. Without hesitation, he fire round after round, as if he were showing off. Sean can't believe his eyes. His dad laughs insanely as he empties the clip. "Man that was good!", his dad says with a smile. "Where'd you learn to shoot like that dad?" "There's a lot of things about your dad that you don't know. By the way, don't tell anyone about this. This is mine and your secret." "Don't worry dad. Your secret is safe with me." As they walk out of the room and back into the first room, the old man stands near the exit. "See you next time old man", his dad says. "Yeah, see you next time", says Sean. His dad exits, but just before Sean can the old man grabs his shoulder and says, "he who has seen death need not worry about opening doors." "What the hell is wrong with you old man, you off your rocker or something?" "Try to ignore, but it's always there. Try to run from it if you dare." Sean pushes the old mans hand off of his shoulder and walks backwards out the door. He trips and falls.

"You ok son?" Thinking it's his dad, Sean laying on his back, opens his eyes to see the bright sun staring back at him. "Are you ok?" With blurred vision, Sean looks at what seems to be his dad looking over top of him. He helps him up and brushes dust of the back of him. "You had me worried for a second there. You got to watch where you're going." "Sean, dazed and confused, stagers to the car, opens the door and gets in. As he shuts the door, he looks over to his dad, whom quickly morphs into the Grim Reaper. The doors lock automaticly as Sean screams and tries to get out. "Help! Help!", he yells. The Reaper grabs the steering wheel and puts the car into reverse backing into the middle of the street. As it lets out a roar, the Reaper slams the car into drive and takes off down the road. Sean screams for help as the Reaper smacks his head against the door window.

"Sean! Sean wake up!" He opens his eyes slowly to see his father standing over him. "What happened?", asks Sean. "You tripped and fell. How's your head?", his dad asks. Sean rubs it and says, "ok I guess." His dad helps him up. "Come on. Let's go." They walk to the car and get in. Sean, sitting in the passenger seat, looks over to his dad slowly as if to check to see if he turns into the Reaper. "I'm hungry. Let's get something.", his dad says. He puts the car in reverse and backs out into the road then shifts it into drive and drives away.

A couple of miles down the road, they stop in a run down little diner. They both exit the car and walk in. As Sean enters the diner, he looks around to see only a couple of people in there. "Ya'll sit anywhere ya'll want to.", the waitress behind the counter says. Sean and his walk to their right and sit down in a booth. The waitress walks over and introduces herself. "Hi. My name's Christy. What can I get you two?" As Sean's dad checks her out, He responds with a smile, "I'll have a cheese burger, fries and water." She turns and asks Sean, "and for you?" "I'll have the same." "Ok, be right up." As she turns and walks away, Sean's dad checks her out. "Dad!" "What? I'm still alive you know." Sean turns his head and stares out the window. A vehicle pulls in and two men get out. Both of them look like they are up to no good. "I'll be right back son. I have to take a leak." His dad slides out of the booth and walks into the back. As the two men walk in, Sean watches them. "I thought I told you two never to come in here again!", the waitress shouts. One man pulls out a shot gun and shoots the waitress at point blank range sending her flying over the counter. Sean, shaking like a leaf, ducks under the table. "Go get the money!", one man shouts. Sean covers his head and tries not to make a sound. More shots ring out. A dead silence hits the air for a moment. "Sean? Sean? You can come out now.", his dad says. Sean, still shaking, crawls out from the table and stands up. "Are you ok?", his dad asks. "Yeah." Sean looks around and can not believe his eyes. Both men are lying on the floor in pools of blood with holes in their heads. The other customers stand in the back ground silently. The chef stands on the other side of the counter holding a meat cleaver. "Let's go son." "Wait.", says Sean. "Shouldn't we wait for the cops to arive?" "No.", his dad says. "If the cops find out I did this you won't ever see me again." "Don't worry.", says the chef. "We'll take care of

this. Just leave me the gun." He hands him the gun and says, "Thanks."
"No. Thank you." "Let's go Sean." They exit the diner. Sean grabs
the door handle of the car and looks back at the diner. His eyes get
really big. He see the Reaper collecting the dead. As he opens his
robe, the dead walk into him, disappearing one by one. Sean climbs
in the car and slams the door. "Come on dad. Start the car." His dad
starts the car and tears out of the parking lot. "You mind telling me
what that was all about.", asks Sean. "My guns aren't legal. That's
all I can tell you for right now." Sean doesn't ask anymore questions.
"I trust you dad." "I know you do son." "Let's get back to the house. I
need to disguss something with you.", his dad says.

Back at the house, Sean sit on the sofa, while his dad sits in a
chair across from him. "There's something you need to know. I got a
phone call from your mother. She told me that Jessica killed herself.
They found her in her room with a needle sticking out of her arm. I'm
sorry to be the one to tell you this." Sean just sits there with a blank
look on his face. "It's ok if you want to cry. I understand.", says his
dad. "Did you know that she did drugs?" "No.", replies Sean. "Is there
anything you want to tell me?", his dad asks. "I know what really
happened to Jessica." "Go on. I'm listening." "Patricia did it." "How
do you know this?" "She told me. She said she would kill me if I told."
His dad sits there wondering if Sean's telling the truth. "Do you have
proof?" "No.", says Sean. Sean begins to tell his dad the conversation
he and Patricia had. "Why would I tell you this if I didn't have to?"
"It's ok son. I believe you. One things for sure though, if you go back
home to your mother you'll have to face Patricia." "Can't I just live
here with you?" "Well, I guess so, but it's up to your mother, at least
until you turn eighteen." "Thanks dad." Sean hugs his dad and walks
back to his room. He opens the door and sits on the bed. He pulls out
his wallet and pulls out a picture of Jessica. Tears come to his eyes as
he presses the picture to his face. His dad stands in the doorway and
watches Sean as he falls apart.

The next day, Sean's dad knocks on his door. "Get up son." Sean,
dazed, gets up out of bed and puts his clothes on. He walks out of his
room and proceeds into the kitchen. He sits down at the table, while
his dad gives him a plate of food. "You sleep ok?", his dad asks.

"Yeah.", Sean replies. "Todays a new day. We're gonna get on with our lives and not think about the past.", says his dad. "I don't know about you dad, but I'm worried about what I'm going to do about Patricia." "You want me to take care of her?" "What do you mean?" "I can make her disappear if you want me to." "No dad. I don't want to hurt her. I just wish that I could erase it all." "Be careful what you wish for son. You might just get it. Now eat up. I want to show you something." "I dont' know if I have the strenght today dad." "Trust me son. You're gonna like this."

In the back yard, Sean and his dad walk to the tool shed. "Follow me. I want to show you something." They enter the small shed as his dad shuts the door behind them and locks it. He puts his hands on Sean's shoulders and say, "What I'm about to show you you can not tell anyone." He reaches over and pushes a button on the wall. Sean steps back as part of the back wall opens up and a strange green neon glow apears. "Follow me.", his dad says. They walk down some stairs and into a clean looking room that's filled with all kinds of guns. "What the hell dad?!" "You can never be too prepared son. I need to ask you a very important question. Do you want to live forever?" "What kind of question is that?" "Are you afraid of death?" Sean doesn't speak. He just stares at his dad. "I think it's time you learned a little about your dad. When you were little, your mom and I had a big fight so I left. I walked out of the house and got into my car. I had been drinking and didn't know where I was going. I pulled up to a stop light, but decided to keep on going. I was struck by another car and was ejected. As I lay on the ground I was blacking in and out. I looked over to the other car and saw this "thing" dressed in a black robe caring a big curvey blade. As the driver from the car walked toward the "thing", the driver disappeared, as if the "thing" had swallowed him. Then the "thing" turned toward me, but began to flicker on and off like a light bulb. There was a power line down between me and "it". "It" tried to get to me, but it wouldn't come past the power line. The "black thing" finally dissappeared as I sat there and waited for the paramedics to arrive. I was charged with drunk driving and man slaughter and was sent to prison for five years. While I was in there, I never forgot what I saw that night. I tried to read every book I could that talked about ghost or the super natural.

I wanted to know what the hell I saw. I began to see things that I couldn't explain. I saw an inmate get stabbed to death and watched this "thing" come get him like the boogyman or something. When I got out I moved here and began building a weapon. I thought about the downed powerline and why the "thing" didn't like it." Sean's dad walks over to a small table where a sheet is covering something. He pulls the sheet back, exposing what looks like a futuristic rifle. He reaches down and picks it up with both hands. As he shows it to Sean, Sean backs up. "Don't be afraid.", his dad says. "What is it?", asks Sean. "I call it, "The Lightning rod". "What does it do?" "It harnesses a bolt of lightning so you can shoot it. It can stay loaded for a long time." "So, why did you build it?" "One of us is gonna use it to get rid of that "thing". "What do you mean, one of us?" "If you or I see that "thing" again we can destroy it by shooting it. "How did you know I can see it?", asks Sean. "I saw that look in your eyes when we were at the diner. Hell, you probably saw "it" when you were in your coma." Sean turns around and walks out of the shed. His dad follows. "Sean wait." "That gun ain't gonna kill "it". You can't kill somethings that already dead." Sean continues to walk inside the house as his dad stops just outside the door. He turns around and walks back into the shed.

Sean, sitting on the side of his bed, thinks about what his dad has just told him. He hears the back door open and shut as his dad walk back inside and to his bedroom door. With the door open, his dad stands staring at him. "What's going through your mind right now son?" "Everything.", Sean replies. "Look, you shouldn't worry about anything. As long as we stick together it can't get us.", his dad says. "You don't get it dad. This "thing" can't be stopped. Once we die, it comes for us." His dad walks over and sits down beside him. "We can't just give up. Maybe we can reason with it." "I doubt that dad." "Well, I've got to go out for a little bit. You stay here and chill out for a while. Watch some t.v. or something." His dad gets up and walks out of the room. Sean grabs his head phones and puts them on. He then turns his "IPOD" on and lays back, closing his eyes and drifting off to sleep. There's a knock on the front door. Sean opens his eyes and pulls the earphones from his head. He hears the knock again. This time, he gets off his bed and walks out of his room, down the hall and to the front door. He grabs the knob slowly and opens it. "Hey Sean!", a small voice says. Sean can't believe his eyes. It's Patricia. She pulls a gun out from her purse and shoots Sean six times.

"AHHHH!", Sean screams. He opens his eyes, still laying in his bed and still wearing his earphones. It was just a dream. Sweat dribbles from his forehead. He wipes it away as he gets off the bed and walks back into the kitchen. He grabs a glass from a cabinet and runs water into it. As he drinks it, there is a knock at the door. He slowly puts the glass into the sink and walks over to the door. He opens the door. "Hey little brother!", says Adam. "What are you doing here?", Sean asks with excitment. "I've come to see how you're doing. Dad just picked me up from the airport. He's out there at the car right now getting my luggage. Well, aren't you gonna let me in?" "Oh, yeah. Sorry. Come on in." As Adam is looking at Sean, he asks, "You ok man? You look like you've seen a ghost or something." Sean and Adam go into Sean's room as their dad struggles outside with luggage. "Damn it Adam, you couldv'e given me a hand.

"So how you doin?", asks Adam. "Ok. I guess. I've been wanting to talk to you about what happened." "What do you mean?" "When I was in my coma, did you see me?" "Of course, I was at the hospital alot." "No. I mean other than there." "I'm not sure I follow." "Like at the school, when you got in that fight with those guys . . ." "Wait. How did you know about that?" "I was there, remember? You looked right at me." "Sorry dude. Can't help you there. You want to lay down or something, because you're freaking me out man." "No. Just forget it." Sean walks out of his room and into the den where his dad is sitting in his chair and watching t.v.. Sean sits down on the sofa as Adam does the same. "Whatcha watchin pops?", asks Adam. "The news.", says his dad. A video of the war in the gulf is shown as a news anchor talks about it. "For the past couple of days, our troops have been fighting to keep the peace in the gulf. Hopefully, they will be coming home soon." As soldiers run around, the Reaper is also seen collecting the dead. This startles Sean and his dad as they look at each other. His dad quickly turns the channel to some hot rod show. "Now this is more like it.", says Adam. His dad looks at him, thankful that he doesn't see the Reaper as well. They continue watching until the late of the night.

The light from Sean's bedroom window peaks in through the curtains and catches Sean's eyes. "Mmmm.", he moans, as he turns over. His dad's voice is heard in the background. "Sean. You and your brother want to go with me to the store?" "Yeah.", Sean shouts. "Well, get up then." "Alright." Sean gets out of bed and puts his clothes on. He then proceeds out of his room and to the kitchen. His dad and brother stand waiting. "Let's go.", his dad says. The walk out the front door with Sean bringing up the rear and shutting the door behind him. "Morning!", his dad says to the neighbor who's coughing really bad. "Cough. Morning.", the old woman says. "Man, she looks like crap.", says Adam. "Yeah. She must have the flu or something.", says his dad. All three get into the car. Sean, sitting in the back seat, keeps looking at the old woman. She turns and walks back into the house. The Grim Reaper appears behind her, but doesn't follow. Sean's eyes grow big and he starts breathing faster. The Reaper turns toward Sean and lets out a roar. "Sean!", his dad shouts. "Wake up. You're having a dream." "What happened?", Sean asks. "You passed out or something.", says Adam. "Are you ok son?" "I'm fine dad." His dad turns back around in his seat and backs out of the driveway. He then puts the car in drive and takes off.

The car pulls into the store parking lot and parks in front. All three exit the car and walk to the door. A woman dressed in a skimpy outfit stands outside bothering customers. "Come on. Take me home with you.", she says. "Get the hell away from me.", one guy replies. Just before Sean and Adam reach her, Adam says, "Hey Sean, watch this." "Hey baby. How you doin?" "Hey fatty. You got any money?" "What? Forget you Biatch!" He continues to walk passed her and into the store. She makes eye contact with Sean, but doesn't say a word. Sean doesn't say anything either. He just follows Adam into the store. "You guys just get what you want.", his dad says. All three go down seperate aisles. Sean enters one with candy. As he stands there, a little kid is heard on the next aisle over coughing. Sean doesn't think much of it and continues on walking. The coughing gets worse and lowder the more Sean ignores it. He decides to investigate so he walks around the corner to find a little boy coughing, while standing and holding hands with the Grim Reaper. Sean, startled, pretends he doesn't see it and turns around. He walks fast the other way, but just as he reaches the end of the aisle, he runs into Adam. Everything that Adam is carrying flies out of his arms and hits the ground. "Damn dude. Can't you watch where you're going?", yells Adam. About this time, their dad walks up and says, "What happened?" "Nothing.", both boys say at the same time. Their dad shakes his head and walks up to the counter to pay. Sean looks back down the aisle, but there is no one there, not even the little boy.

Back in the car, Sean sits in the back seat and stares at the girl standing just outside of the store. She keeps trying to get guys to take her home as they walk by. As his dad starts to drive off, the girl pauses for a brief second to look at him. She gives a bad look and then looks the other way. "How would you like to have a go with that?", asks Adam, being smart. "There's something weird about that girl.", says Sean. "Yeah", his dad says. "I can sense it, too." "What are ya'll talking about?", asks Adam. "She's just a "pro". That's all." Sean's dad looks at him in the rear view mirror. Sean sits back in his seat and looks out the window as the car drives off down the street.

Back at the store, Sean walks down the candy aisle. He grabs a bag of his favorite candy and walks over to the refrigerated soda. He opens a door and pulls out a flavored water. As he looks around to check to see if anyone is looking, he opens the top and takes a couple of swigs. He puts the cap back on and shoves the drink back where it came from. Turns out the owner of the store had an encounter with the girl standing outside of it, but when he didn't pay up she decided to get revenge on him. She knew what his favorite drink was, so she simply spiked it and returned it back on the shelf. Unfortunately, Sean got to it first.

The car pulls into the driveway and stops. Sean gets out, as Adam and his father follow. "Aren't you gonna help with the groceries?", his dad asks, as Sean takes off and runs up to the front door. He takes out his door key and fumbles trying to get it in the hole. "Come on damnit!" He just about breaks down the door as he falls in. He picks himself up, leaving the key in the door and rushes to the bathroom. He slams the door behind him and does everything he can to unbuckle his belt. His pants fall to the ground and he sits down on the toilet. As he paints the inside of the bucket, he begins to feel nautious. With the tub sitting in front of him, he leans over and projectile vomits. "knock. Knock. Hey Sean are you ok?", asks Adam. "Go away." "Whatever.", says Adam, as he turns and walks back into the kitchen. "What wrong with your brother?" "I think he's sick. He's in there throwing up." "Did he eat anything while we were at the store?" "I don't think so." "I'll go check on him." His dad walks down the hall and knocks on the door. "Sean. You ok?" "Just go away." "Do you need me to take you to the Hospital?" "No." "Alright. I'll be right here if you need me." His dad stands outside the door until Sean comes out. After awhile, Sean finally opens the door. "You look bad. Come on. Let's lay down." He supports Sean and walks him to his room. He lays him on the bed and covers him up with a small blanket. "I'll bring you back some water." As his dad leaves the room, Adam pears around the corner. "You ok man?" "Yeah", Sean wispers. "What happened?", ask Adam. "I don't know. One minute I'm fine, the next I'm not." "Maybe it's just the flu.", says Adam. "I hope not." "I hope I don't get it. I can't afford to lose anymore weight.", says Adam trying not to laugh. Sean lays there in pain, grabbing his stomach and moaning. His dad walks back in with a glass of water and some medicine. He hands it to Sean as he takes it. "Just rest Sean.", his dad says. He and Adam turn and leave the room. Sean turns over on his side in agony and stares at the floor. He begins to hallucinate as the carpet turns into maggots. Frightened, he closes his eyes quickly for a few seconds and then reopens them. The maggots are gone and all he sees is carpet. He takes deep breaths and turns back over onto his back and closes his eyes.

A voice is heard in the background. "Ssssseeeeeaaaaannnnn." Sean runs down a dark hallway in slow motion. He hears the voice again, except this time the voice is lowder. "Sssseeaaannn!" While running, he looks back to see nothing but smoke. As he looks forward, the Grim Reaper appears behind him, floating closely to the ceiling with his arm spread outward and holding the giant sythe in his right hand. Sean's dad appears down the hall, waving him to "come on!" As he runs past his dad, his dad pulls out the "Lightening Rod" from behind him. "Eat one point twenty-one gigawatts." Just as he fires it up, Sean opens his eyes. He sits up in bed and rubs the sweat off his face. He rubs his eyes so much that when he stops he tries to look around, but is blind for a couple of seconds. As his vision restores, he sees Jessica sitting at the end of his bed staring at him with tears in her eyes. "Jessica?" "I'm sorry Sean. I . . ." There's a bang on the door. She disappears and the banging stops. "What the hell was that?", he thinks to himself.

Adam and his dad sit in the den watching television. Adam lays back on the sofa as he tries to throw popcorn into his mouth. "Damn it Adam. You're making a mess.", his dad says. Adam brushes off the crumbs while saying, "sorry dad."

Ran begins to hit the window as thunder is heard lightly off in the distance. "I'll be right back son." Adam's dad gets out of his chair and grabs his coat hanging by the front door. He walks to the back door that's right beside Sean's room. Sean, startled by the door slamming, leans over and looks out the window and watches his dad walk to the shed. Knowing and interested in what his dad is about to do, he slowly gets out of bed and walks barefoot out of his room and around the corner to the back door. He stands and watches through the glass. It's no time before his dad reappears walking out of the shed with the weapon that he had made. He looks around to see if anyone is watching. He then, clicks a switch on the weapon and a foot long spike pokes out the rear of it. Just before he stabs it into the ground he looks up at Sean and grins. He thrusts it in the ground and runs back to the shed, waiting to see what's going to happen. The ground is so wet that the weapon doesn't stay in place. It starts to fall over as Sean opens the door and runs outside to catch it. He falls in the mud face first. As he picks himself up, he stands covered in mud, but holding the weapon. "Sean!" "It's ok dad. I caught it." His dad runs out to him, but before he can get to him Sean is struck by lightning. It passes through him and into the weapon, blowing him back ten feet. He lies on the ground unconscious as his dad rushes over to him yelling his name. "Sean! Oh no! What have I done?" He picks him up, leaving the weapon on the ground and goes back into the house. He lays him on his bed and tries to wake him up. Adam walks in, "what

45

happened dad?" "He got hit by lightning.", his dad says in tears. "I'll call the paramedics.", says Adam. He turns around and runs back into the kitchen and grabs the phone. Sean's dad listens close to see if he is breathing. He is, but barely. His dad smiles and wipes the tears from his eyes as he looks around the room as if to be looking for the Reaper. "Mmmm.", says Sean. "Sean. Can you hear me? It's ok. It's me. Dad." Sean slowly opens his eyes. "Oh my God.", his dad says. "Your eyes!" Sean had been hit with so much electricity that his eyes were nothing, but blue light. He blinks a couple of times and the light goes out. His eyes then go back to normal. Adam comes running back in. "I called the paramedics. They're on their way." "How do you feel son?" "Great actually." Sean sits up and smiles. His dad smiles back at him, while Adam confused yells, "will someone please tell me what the hell is going on?" "I think everything's going to be ok. When the paramedics get here we'll tell them it was a false alarm." Sean looks at Adam and says, "I'm ok dude, just feel a little tingly that's all." His dad kind of giggles as he walks past Adam and out of the room. "That's not funny dad.", Adam says. "I don't even feel sick anymore." Adam walks out of the room shutting the door behind him. Sean lays back down in the bed with his hair smoking and closes his eyes. His dad is seen out the window, picking up the loaded weapon and running through the rain back to the shed.

Light flashes before Sean's eyes, as he drifts off to sleep and into dream world. He sees himself walking out of the house and into the back yard. The lightning strikes him sending a shock throughout his body. He wakes up to find himself engulfed in flames and his bed as well. The flames don't hurt him, but he screams anyway. His dad comes rushing in as well as his brother. "Oh my God!", his dad yells. He runs back into the kitchen where he grabs a small fire extinguisher and runs back into Sean's room. "Move Adam!" Almost knocking Adam down, he rushes by him and pulls the pin from the extinguisher. He points it toward Sean, but just as he does, Sean yells, "Wait dad!". His dad pauses and Sean relaxes himself. He breathes a couple of times as the flames begin to die down. His body is left untouched by the flames as well as his clothes. "What the hell was that Sean?", asks Adam. "Yeah and what is that smell?", his dad asks. "It smells like some kind of electrical smell." Sean is drenched in what looks like sweat, but isn't. "I think some kind of fuel is coming from my body. It doesn't taste like sweat. It actually burns my tongue a little." His dad grabs his arm and licks it. He immediately spits it out. "That taste like battery acid." "What's wrong with me dad?" "I don't know son, but I'll take you to the hospital."

All three arrive at the hospital around eight o'clock at night. They exit the car and walk inside. Adam walks over to a chair in the waiting room and sits down. Sean and his dad walk up to the front desk. A cute brown haired girl sits behind it. "Hello. How may I help you?" "My son needs to be looked over. He was hit by lightning and I just want to make sure nothing is wrong with him." She looks over his shoulder and looks Sean up and down. "Doesn't look like anything is wrong with him." She hands his dad a form to fill out. "Just fill this out and have a seat in the lounge." His dad takes the form and walks into the lounge where Adam sits reading a magazine. Sean sits beside of Adam and begins to bite his finger nails. "You're not nervous are?", a voice asks. Sean looks behind himself and sees an old man in a hospital rob sitting in a chair. "I wouldn't be so nervous if I were you. We all have to die sometime, might as well except it." Sean whispers to the man. "Are you dead?" The man laughs and says, "Not yet. I'm in purgatory." Sean turns back around and closes his eyes. "Sean?" He opens his eyes to see the doctor standing in front of him. "I'm doctor Reuben. Follow me please." Sean stands up and looks back at the old man, but he is gone. "Ok Sean. Says here you got hit by lightning, but I don't see any burn marks. How do you feel?" "Ok. I guess." "I'm going to listen to your heart beat." He grabs his stethoscope and puts it on Sean's chest. "Well, you sound ok. Are you experiencing any dizziness or blurred vision?" "No." "Hmm. Well, I don't see anything wrong with you. I'll be right back." The doctor leaves the room as Sean waits. Five minutes later, the doctor steps back in. "Ok Sean. You're free to go." Sean walks out of the room and down the hallway. Adam and his dad stand waiting for him. "How'd it go?", his dad asks. "He couldn't find anything. It was a waste of time. Let's just go home." Just as they reach the doors, Sean passes out and falls to the ground. "No! Sean!", his dad yells.

Seans eyes roll back into his head, as he goes in and out of consciousness. He sees his dad holding him in his arms and yelling his name. The Reaper appears behind his dad, but stands waiting. Seans dad takes a sniff. "Do you smell that?", he asks. "Dad drop him quick!", yells Adam. He does, but Sean doesn't hit the ground. He levitates about an inch above the floor. He lights up like a match as everyone in the room backs away. He then throws his arms up toward the ceiling sending lightning through them and hitting the Reaper. The Reaper is thrown across the room and vanishes into thin air. Sean's flames instantly go out as he hits the floor. The sprinklers come on and the hospital staff run away. His dad picks him up and carries him out to the car. Adam follows. "Wait!", the doctor yells. His dad turns around and says, "You forget about what you have seen today." The doctor says nothing, just stares in disbelief. His dad turns around and says, "come on Adam. You drive." He hands him the keys and keeps on walking to the car. He puts Sean in the back seat and then gets in the passenger. Adams hops in the driver's side and closes the door. He starts the car and takes off. On the way home, Adam looks in the rear view mirror at Sean and then over to his dad. "Dad you mind telling me what is going on." "I don't know son, but right now Sean needs us more than anything." "What he did back there, that wasn't human.", says Adam. "People just don't levitate and shoot electricity out of there bodies." "I don't have any answers for you Adam. I'm just as clueless as you." The car pulls into the drive. Adam shuts it off and gives the keys to his dad. "Do you need any help with him?", asks Adam. "No. I've got him." Adam runs up to the front door and opens it. He stands holding it open for his dad. His dad picks Sean up in his arms and carries him in. "Go and get me a wash cloth and a towel", his dad says. He takes him into the bathroom and sits him on the toilet. He puts his hands on Sean's face and looks him in the eyes. "Sean." Sean looks at him with a blank stare. "You ok?", his dad asks. "Yeah", says Sean. "I just need to catch my breath." "Get in the shower. You'll feel a lot better." "Alright." His dad walks out as Adam walks in. "Here's a wash cloth and a towel.", he says, as he hands them to Sean. "You gonna be ok?" "Yeah". "Me and dad will be right out side the door if you need us." "Ok." Adam turns around and walks out and close the door behind him. Sean turns the water on in the tub and lets it fill up. He then takes his clothes off and gets in slowly. The hot water burns one foot at a time. He reaches over and turns on the cold water to bring the temperature down. He then eases down in the tub. With one foot, he reaches up and turns off the water. He lays back and relaxes. With the water so warm, it relaxes him so much that it puts him to sleep. He begins to slip down underneath the water until he is completely submerged. He takes the water in as it fills up his lungs. The water begins to glow a bright red orange color and then comes to a boil. Flames appear on top of the water and melt the shower curtain. The Grim Reaper stands on the outside of the tub, while the melted curtain drips onto his shreaded black robe. He reaches down in the water and pulls Sean's soul up out of it. He opens his black robe, but just before he can take Sean, Sean's dad kicks the bathroom door open. The Reaper turns his head toward him and lets out a roar. "Rrrrooooaaarrr!" "Put my son down!", his dad yells, as he holds the "Lightning Rod" in his hands. He raises it and aims it toward the Reaper. The Reaper lets Sean's soul go as it falls back into his body. He then turns toward his dad and lunges at him. His dad fires the weapon and lights up the whole room. The light could be seen out the window across the neighborhood. When it is all over, the Reaper is gone and Sean's dad stands trembling, still holding the weapon in both hands. He looks over at the tub and drops the weapon on the ground. He runs to the side of the tub and kneels down. He reaches in and pulls Sean's lifeless body out of the water. Sean's soul stands behind his dad. Adam stands in the doorway as a tear runs down his cheek. While holding Sean, his dad lets out a sufering yell.

"Ashes to ashes, dust to dust.", the preacher says. Everyone's gathered around Sean's casket. His mother stands weeping, as well as his dad and brother. After all is said and done, everyone turns and walks away. Sean stands looking down at his casket. He looks up and is startled by the Reaper standing on the other side. This time, the Reaper just stands and does nothing. "What?!", yells Sean. "You want my soul? Well, here it is." The Repear floats through the casket quickly, but stops just before Sean. They stare each other down, as if they were in a boxing match. "So make your move", says Sean. The Reaper opens its giant robe and a bright white light presents itself and Sean is captivated by it. Sean enters the Reaper with no hesitation. The Reaper closes his robe and vanishes.

Back in the bathroom, "Cough, cough!". Sean spits up water out of his lungs. His dad smiles. "Sean!" He leans him over to let the water out. Adam stands in the doorway in disbelief knowing that his brother should be dead. Sean opens his eyes and says, "He's real." "Who Sean?", asks his dad. "God", he says. "I was there. I saw him." Sean tries to catch his breath. His dad covers him with a blanket and helps him up. "What did he look like?", asks Adam. "Like Jesus?" Sean just smiles. His dad helps him to his room where Sean lays down on his bed. Adam walks in behind him. "Well you gonna tell me or what?" "I guess it was Jesus. I don't think it was anyone else." "Hmm", says Adam. His dad turns to him and says, "Let your brother rest. I don't know how much he can stand, but it can't be much more. Do you want me to leave Sean?" "It's ok dad. I'm not afraid now. God is with me." He smiles and winks. His eyes glow in and out that strange, blue color again. His dad smiles back and turns arounds and walks out. Sean, with a smile on his face, lays and stares at the ceiling. He daydreams of where he has been, what he has done and what he is capable of.

As he daydreams, he pictures himself back at that last moment with the Grim Reaper. It opens its robe and the bright light is exposed. Sean's eyes are large and can't believe what he is seeing. He sees big white clouds and a golden staircase. As he proceeds to walk inside, he looks back just as the robe is closing. He then looks forward and starts to walk toward the staircase. Suddenly, a figure appears. It's a man dressed in a long white robe, with long white hair and beard. "Hello my son. Welcome. We've been expecting you." "You have?", asks Sean. "Yes, but we won't you to return." "Why?" "You are special and you have just begun." Sean looks at the man with a strange look. "What do you mean special?" "I think you know. Do you remember being hit by lightning?" "Yeah. So what?" "Well, you are now . . . the Lightning Rod!" Sean bust out laughing, "ha ha ha!" "I'm glad you think it's funny. Now I'm going to show you how to use it." Sean pauses and the man points at him. Sean's arms raise as electricity flows out of them. He levitates just enough to get his feet off the ground. His hair stands up as well. "Hey, put me down old man!" The man laughs. "Ha ha ha!" "I mean it! Put me down!", yells Sean. The man quickly lowers his arm and Sean falls to the floor, bursting into flames. As he is on fire, he looks up at the man. The man says, "You can control the flames with your anger and you might want to hurry, because there is not suppose to be fire in heaven." Sean tries calming himself as his flames dissipate. "Now get up and go back where you came from." "Won't I still be dead?" "Don't worry. You won't be.", the man says as he slowly disappears. Sean turns around and starts walking. He slowly vanishes himself and then wakes up in his dad's arms in the bathroom.

The next morning, Sean's dad rolls over in bed and opens his eyes. He stares at the digital clock, but it isn' t on. He reaches over and grabs his watch from the night stand beside the bed. The watch reads noon. "What the hell?", he says. He gets up out of bed and puts his clothes on. The house is dem and silent. He looks into Adam's room to see him still lying in bed. "Adam!" "Hmm?" "Get up." He then walks down the hall to Sean's room. A blue glow is seen from underneath the door. His dad knocks on the door. "Knock knock." There is no answer. "You ok Sean?" Still, there is no answer. He grabs the knob and turns it slowly. He then opens the door as the light gets brighter. Sean lays on his bed, floating and glowing a light blue light. His dad pauses and watches him. Adam walks by the door and glances in quickly, but keeps on walking. He then turns around and comes flying in and stands beside his dad. They both watch Sean for what seems forever. "This is the coolest thing I've ever seen", says Adam. "I know", his dad says. "Should we wake him?", asks Adam. "No. He might burn the whole house down if we do." "We shouldn't leave him though." "We're not. We're gonna stay right here until he wakes." Adam and his dad stay in Sean's room until he wakes hours later. By this time, he lays on his bed covered up in a ball and shivering. "It's cold in here", he mumbles. His dad grabs a blanket and throws it over him. Sean finally wakes up, refreshed and recharged. "Morning guys." "Morning", they both say. Sean leans up in his bed and stretches. "You want a glass of water Sean?" His dad turns toward Adam and says, "Go get him a glass of water". Adam walks out of the room and into the kitchen. He walks back in with the glass of water and gives it to Sean. "Here you go". Sean takes it and gulps it to the last drop. He then hands the glass to his dad. "How do you feel today son?" Sean pauses for a moment . . . "I feel good". "Sean. You were floating above your bed and glowing. You mind explaining that to me?" "I was? I can't explain it." "Sean, you have some sort of powers inside you. If this gets out we might see people that want to hurt you. You need to keep this on the down low." "I dreamed that I was flying. I felt so relaxed." "I have to go to work today Sean. Are you going to be ok for awhile?" "Don't worry about me dad." "Adam, watch out for your brother while I'm gone." "Sure dad." Their dad walks out of the room and out the front door. Adam walks over and sits down on Sean's bed. "So, I guess since dad's gone I can tell you now. I did see your soul walking around when you were in your coma." "Why didn't you tell me the truth earlier?" "I don't know. I guess I didn't want to think that I was a freak, but now that I know you can levitate I don't feel so weird." "You and I are different so like dad said we have to be careful", says Sean. "I've seen other dead people, too", says Adam. "Most of them I don't even know. I pretend that I don't see them."

Later on, their dad comes home from work. As he walks through the front door, Sean and Adam sit in the living room watching television. "Hey boys." "Hey dad", they both say. "Ya'll hungry? I brought some chicken." Sean and Adam get up and walk over to the kitchen. All three sit down at the table and eat. They sit and talk about this and that when there is a knock on the door. Their dad gets up from his chair and walks over to the door. As he opens it, a man dressed in a black suit, dark sunglasses and a tie stands with about a dozen men behind him dressed the same way. "We know about your son and his ability. May I come in?" "Sure", their dad says. He turns to his side and lets the man in. He walks in calmly and sits down at the table across from Sean. Sean's dad stands behind him, but doesn't say anything. The man speaks. "We know everything about you Sean. We know . . . everything." Sean slowly gets up from his chair. The man stands as well. Sean darts from the kitchen and out the back door. The man follows. Sean's dad and Adam can't do anything, but watch. "Grab him!", the man shouts. As Sean exits the house, he is surrounded by men with tazors. They zap Sean and he falls to the ground. He cries out in agony. "Ahhhh!" They zap him over and over. Sean's dad steps out of the house. "Leave him alone you bastards!" They hold him back as he fights. The man walks over to Sean as he lay flat in the mud. It has begun to rain, soaking the ground even more. The man pulls Sean over onto his back with his foot. Sean gasps for air. The rain pours on his face and he blink and squints uncontrolably. The man bends over and says to Sean, "it is useless to resist us. You are to weak." Sean whispers something, but the man can't hear him. The man gets closer to Sean. "Sorry. I didn't catch that." Sean repeats himself, "thanks for the recharge." The man's eyes enlarge as a bright blue light shines on his face. A strong smell fills the air making everyone cover their noses. The wind begins to blow. Sean rises to his feet. Electricity flows from his body. He breathes deeply and raises his arms to his side. Before everyone can run away, Sean shocks them all. Lightning strikes from the skies several times on the ground all around Sean. He yells out and looks upward. A huge shockwave is sent throughout the neighborhood knocking out all power. Sean falls to the ground and passes out. When it is over no one remains except Sean, Adam and his dad. The rest of the men are piles of ash. Adam and his dad rush over to Sean. His dad supports his head. "Sean!", his dad yells. They carry him into the house and lay him on the couch in the lving room. "Go get me a towel", he says to Adam. Adam runs in the back as his dad tries to get Sean to wake up. "Sean. Can you hear me?" Sean opens his eyes just enough to see. "Where am I?", he asks. "You're ok. You're safe." Adam walks up with a towel and gives it to his dad. He puts it around Sean. "I want you boys to listen. We can't stay here. If we do they will find us and kill us." Sean is clueless. "Adam. Go pack your bag. I'll go pack Sean's. Sean you just relax." Adam takes off to his room and his dad goes to his. Looking through Sean's eyes, he sees nothing but blue. He looks down at his hands and they are tender and red. He wonders to himself what just happened. Several minutes later, his dad and Adam walk back in. "Can you get up son?" Sean raises up slowly. "I'm so weak." "Come on. Adam get the door", he says. They walk out the front door as Adam closes it behind him. They get in the car and their dad puts the key in the ignition. He tries to start the car, but nothing happens. He then looks over to Sean in the passenger seat who is about past out again. He reaches down and grabs his hand. He then connects his hand to the key. The car starts right up. Adam and his dad laugh. "Thanks son", he says to Sean as he backs out of the driveway.

"Dad. Where are we going?", asks Adam. "Far away from here. Don't worry. I have another place you guys don't know about. We have to be on the look out for those men though. There's probably alot more where they came from." They head for the mountains just outside of town. As they drive down a long stretch of a highway you can see the small town off in the distance. Adam's dad turns on the radio. A woman says, "Police are looking for three men that are wanted for questioning in at least a dozen muders that happened just hours ago. If you have any info about this please contact the authorities immediately." Adam's dad turns the radio off. "What the hell dad? They're trying to pin that on us?" Sean wakes up and looks over at his dad. Then he looks out the front window. "Where are we going?" "We're going to a safe place. I don't want to say too much, because they might be listening to us. We need to get some supplies." They stop off at a small gas station just down the road. All three exit the car and go inside. Inside the gas station a clerk asks, "How you folks doing today?" No one replies. "Get some good stuff to eat guys", says their dad. Both boys walks seperate ways. A television is on behind the counter. The clerk sits and watches it. Adam and Sean both walk up at the same time with tons of can food in hand. They lay everthing on the counter as the clerk starts stuffing everything in bags. "Ya'll need a gun?", the clerk asks. They pause and look at him. "I saw the news, but I don't believe it. Don't worry. I won't say anything. I think most of this crap is a conspiracy anyway." Sean and Adam look at each other and grin. "Well, ya'll want the gun or not?" "No thanks", their dad says. "We don't need it." After paying, all three walk out of the gas station and get into the vehicle. They pull out and get back on the road. "You think that crazy old man back there will say anything?", as Adam. "I don't think it matters anymore. I think they know anyway", his dad says. As they reach the edge of the mountains, they pull off onto a almost hidden dirt road. As they drive up the road, Sean looks out the window. A black figure runs behind a tree. "Did ya'll see that?" He looks again, but there is nothing there. The car pulls in front of a log cabin and stops. "Well, here we are", their dad says. Ya'll get the food. I'll go check the house." Sean and Adam walk up to the house with food in both arms. "Did you know about this place?", asks Sean. "No", says Adam. Their dad opens the front door from the outside. He turns around and says, "come on in".

He steps inside as the boys follow. Inside, they look around at how it is decorated like some hunter's lodge. There are stuffed deer on the wall and fish as well. "You boys just put the food in the kitchen on the table. I'll handle the rest." Adam and Sean walk into the kitchen to the right. Their dad closes the front door and turns around. He walks toward the kitchen, but then the door explodes thowing him across the room. Sean and Adam are thrown to the ground as well. Sean, in a daze, looks over at Adam. He is knocked out from hitting his head on the counter above him. Sean then looks over to his dad who is also knocked out from the blast. Sean is confused, but angry. He bleeds from his head and mouth. He tries standing up, but falls back down. A man walks in where the front door used to be. He looks just like the first man that came to see them. He stops and stands in front of Sean while looking down at him. "Give up?", the man asks. "Never", says Sean. "I thought I destroyed you?" The man leans over and says, "I'll just keep coming back." As he leans back up more men walk in the house behind the first one. "I didn't get a chance to introduce myself the first time. I have many names, but I like to be called the Reaper." Sean's eyes get really big. The man holds his hand out and smiles. "Come with me Sean." With all his strenght, Sean stands up. He looks over to his brother and dad. "Ok. I'll come with you if you leave them alone." "You have my word", says the Reaper. Sean takes the Reaper's hand. They walk out of the cabin as the other men follow. As soon as they are in the clear, they all disappear at they same time.

Sean, the Reaper and the others fly through what looks like a worm hole in space. "Are you taking me to Heaven again?" The Reaper doesn't say anything. On an odd looking planet, they appear and Sean falls to the ground trying to catch his breath. The Reaper touches him on his shoulder and Sean begins to breath normal. By this time, his looks have changed. He looks around at his surroundings. People dressed in rags walk by looking at him, but they only see him. "Where are we?", asks Sean. "Another place and time." "Why are we here?" "You didn't have a destony on Earth. You have one here." Sean and the Reaper turn toward to one another. "What if I don't want to stay?" "Trust me Sean. I may seem bad, but I'm not. I am only a messenger and guider. Besides, there is something here special just for you." The Reaper points over Sean's shoulder and he turns around. A beautiful girl walks by and smiles. Sean turns back around, but the Reaper and his men are gone, but one. The man looks up at Sean. "Who are you?", Sean asks. "I am your Shadow. Where you go I will follow, but I won't be seen by anyone, but you." "I see", says Sean. Sean turns around and starts walking into what looks like an ancient village. The Shadow follows.

Looking throught the eyes of Sean's dad, he sees the cabin is a mess. He looks over and sees Adam lying on the ground and bleeding. Adam opens his eyes slowly. His dad kneels down beside of him. "Are you ok son?" "Yeah. I'm alright. Ahh. My head", he says as he grabs it. "Were's your brother? Sean!", he yells. "He was right here. Maybe he's in the back." "You stay here. I'm going to look", his dad says. He gets up and runs into the back of the cabin. Adam picks himself up off the floor. His dad comes walking back in. "He's vanished", he says as he looks around the room. "What the hell caused this mess? It looks like the front door exploded." "You don't think those men took him do ya?" "I don't know, but for right now let's just stay here till things blow over." "Aren't you worried about Sean?" "Sean can take care of himself better than I can. If he is with them it's because he let them take him. Now come on. Help me clean up this mess."

Sean walks down a busy street filled with people. "Won't they see how different I am with the clothes I am wearing?", he asks the shadow. "Don't worry. I can fix that." With one wave of his hand, the shadow transforms Sean's clothes into rags just like everyone elses. "Wow! That was cool. What else can you do?" "I am very limited in what I can do, but you hold the key." "So what is it that I'm supposed to do?" "I don't know. I'm just here to shadow you." Sean enters a tavern filled with nasty looking men and women. He is stared at as he walks up to the bar. "You not from around here are ya?", the bartender says. "Nope", replies Sean. "Want something to drink?" "Sure. Whatcha got?" "In here we serve water." "Ain't you got anything stronger?", asks Sean. The bartender laughs and says, "Anything stonger and we'll have to dig you a grave." A couple of men sitting at the bar laugh as well. "Fine then. I'll take one." The Shadow leans up against a wall watching. The bartender pours the water for Sean into a small shot glass. Sean picks it up and swigs the whole thing. He puts the glass down with no problem. The rest of the patrons look at him with astonishment. "What? It's just water." "What did you say your name was?", the bartender asks. Sean looks over to the shadow. The shadow shrugs his shoulders. Sean looks back at the bartender and says, "I'm the Lightning Rod." He turns around and walks out of the tavern. The shadow walks behind him and says, "You know you should've used another name." "I don't care", replies Sean. "People know who you are now." Sean stops and turns around. "So what. I'm not trying to hide. If they think they can step to me then let them." Sean turns around and keeps walking. "You really don't know why I'm here with you do you Sean?" Sean stops walking. "I'm here to help you." "Help me with what?" The Shadow points with his finger. "With that." Sean turns around. A large crowd of people walk toward him with fire in their eyes. "What the hell?" "Exactly", the shadow says. Sean panics. "What do I do?" The Shadow stands and waits. The crowd forms a huge fire ball that come flying toward Sean. He crouches down and covers his head. The Shadow steps in and waves his arms, defelecting the fire from Sean. Sean looks up at the shadow. With his back toward Sean, the shadow looks over his shoulders and says, "Don't be afraid Sean." Sean looks deep inside himself and stands up. With anger in his eyes he raises his arms. Lightning comes from everywhere. In a blink of an eye, the crowd turns to dust. Sean lowers his arms. "I don't feel dizzy like I usually do." "It's the atmosphere. It's different here. You did good Sean." A noise is heard from behind. They turn around and the Reaper appears. He walks slowly toward Sean. "Thank you Sean. I didn't think it would be that easy." The girl he saw when he arrived comes running out of the tavern screaming. She runs up to Sean. She falls to the ground crying. "Thank you", she says. "I guess you want here, too huh?", asks Sean. "No. She is yours." The Reaper walk over to the crowd and begins collecting the souls. He opens his rob and one by one they enter. The Shadow walks over to Sean holding the girl. "I'm sorry Sean, but these where people not of this world." Sean looks down at the girl and asks, "and she?" "She is of this world, but if you choose to stay here with her you must convence her about the others." She looks up at Sean with tears in her eyes. "Where do you come from?", she asks. "I come from a place much similar to this one. I do not mean you harm." "Are you a God?" "No. I'm something else." "What is your name?", she asks. "Sean. What is yours?" "I am Lana. Wherever you go I will go." Sean looks up at the Shadow. The Shadow speaks, "If we do I don't know what will happen to her. She might die." Sean looks back down at her and says, "You might die if I take you." "I'm willing to take that chance", she says. Sean helps the Lana up. The shadow lets her see him. It startles her at first. "It's ok", says Sean. "He's with me." The Shadow turns around, waves his arms and opens a worm portal. Sean and Lana step in, but just before the Shadow does he looks back at the Reaper still collecting his souls. He steps through and the portal closes. As all three fly through space, the Shadow looks back at the planet. He grabs Sean's arm with his left hand and with his right hand points it toward the planet. Electricity flows from Sean and through the Shadow. He blasts the planet exploding it into tiny pieces. Sean and Lana have no idea to what has just happened. "That outta keep the Reaper busy", the shadow thinks to himself. They continue to fly through the worm hole until they reach Earth. The shadow brings them right back to the cabin just after Sean was taken by the Reaper before. "Ok Sean. I must leave you now. The Reaper will be back for you." "What about the front door?", Sean asks as he points to the door. The Shadow waves his hand and the door is restored to brand new. The mess is even cleaned up. The Shadow disappears as Sean and the girl go inside the cabin. His dad and Adam lay on the floor. "Dad!", says Sean as he runs over to him. "Hmm. What happened?" Adam wakes up as well. "Ahh. My head." As his dad rises to his feet, he asks, "Who's the girl?" Sean looks at her and smiles. "I found her outside roaming around. I think she's homeless. Heer name is Lana. Can she stay with us?" "I don't know Sean. It might be too risky." Adam walks over. "She's hot! Of course she can stay." "Shut it Adam", his dad says. "She won't be in the way dad. I promise. Besides, I want to take care of her." "Ok, but keep her out of sight. I don't want to get her in trouble as well." Their dad looks at her and asks, "Do you speak english?" "Yes", she replies. "You're not going to be a problem are you?" "No." "Alright. Sean, you and your brother check out the bedrooms and see which ones you want. I will fix us something to eat." Adam walks into a bedroom down the hall on the right and Sean and Lana walk into a bedroom on the left. "I never knew dad had this place", he says looking around. He looks at Lana and asks, "I guess you want to clean yourself up. There's got to be a bathroom in here somewhere." He takes her hand, but just as he does she pulls him back and kisses him. Sean's eyebrows raise with suprise. "What was that for?" "For saving me. I am yours forever." This would scare most guys, but for Sean it was like she was his soulmate. Sean smiles and says, "come on." He takes her out of the room and walks down the hall a couple of steps. "Here's the bathroom." They walk inside. "Let me show you how the shower works." Sean walks over to the shower and turns on the water for her. "There. That should do be warm enough." He turns around and the girl is naked. "Holy shit!", says Sean. "Ok. Um, just step in the shower. The girl smiles. "Ok. There's the soap", Sean points nervously. "I'll be outside of the room if you need anything." He turns and walks out closing the door behind him. "Why are you all sweaty dude?", asks Adam. "Where is that hot girl at?" "She's in the shower", says Sean while trying to catch his breath. "No way dude!", says Adam as he tries to get past Sean. "Just where do you think you're going?" "Come all. She's so hot." "Back off. She's mine", says Sean. "Well if she's yours then why aren't you in there with her?" "Because, she's really needs a bath not someone distracting here." "Whatever man", says Adam as he turns and walks back into the front room. "Sean could you come in here for a minute?", she asks. "Yeah. Sure", he says. He opens the door and walks in. He then shuts the door. "What do you need?" "I need a towel", she says as she wipes the water from her eyes. "Uh. There must be some towels in this", he says as he opens a cabinet. He pulls out a towel and gives it to her. He also tries not to stare. "Why are you so shy?", she asks. "I've never seen anyone as beautiful as you." She smiles and says, "I am yours." Sean smiles as she steps out of the shower with the towel around her. "Come on. I'll see if I have any clothes that you can wear." They both walk out of the bathroom and into Sean's room. He walks over to his dresser and looks inside, but they are empty. "Dad", he shouts. "Yeah". "Do you have anything that Lana can wear?" "I might. Just check in my room." "Come on", he tells her. They both walk into his dad's room and over to a dresser. Sean pulls a drawer out and pulls out a pair of gray sweat pants and a white t-shirt. "This will have to do for now", he says to her. "What is this?", she asks while holding up the pants. "They're called sweat pants. You wear them like my jeans I have on", he says as he points. She drops her towel and puts them on. She then puts the shirt on as well. "How do I look?", she asks. "Hot, I mean good", Sean says nervously. "Why don't we go in the den now and see what dad is doing." As they walk in, Adam as well as his dad's jaws drop. "Are those my sweat pants?", his dad asks. "Yeah. They fit pretty good don't they?", says Sean. Both Adam and his dad nod. "Well, I'm starving. Let's eat", says Sean. "I've made some soup and sandwiches", his dad says. All four walk over to the table and sit down. "Um, dad does this soup have water in it?" "Of course it does." Sean looks at Lana. "I'll just have a sandwich", she says. "Are you sure? There's plenty to go around", his dad says. "Dad, there's something I have to tell you about Lana." "What is it Sean?" "She can't drink too much water. It makes her feel funny." "I'm sorry I don't follow", his dad says. "I just don't like water that's all", Lana says with a smile. "Well, do you like ham?" "I don't know. I've never had it." Adam looks at her and asks, "So what do you eat?" "I like . . ." A bug crawls across the table. She smacks it. "Oh, I'll take care of that", Sean says as he tries to reach for it. She picks it up and eats it. "Ew gross!", says Adam. "You can keep her dude." "Well, I guess being homeless can be rough", their dad says. "Mmm", she exclaims. "Got anymore?" Sean looks at his dad and says, "There's probably more where that came from."

After they are finished eating, Sean takes Lana back into his bedroom. "Ok. After we eat we brush our teeth." He reaches in his backpack and pulls out a tooth brush and paste. They walk out of the room and into the bathroom. Sean turns on the water in the sink. He puts the paste on the brush and puts it in his mouth. He shows her how to brush. He then spits out the paste in the sink and rinses his mouth out with water. "Now your turn", he says. She takes the brush and does the same, but doesn't rinse her mouth out. "Ah! It burns!", She says while grabing her mouth. She turns the water on and rinses her mouth out. She leans back up and wipes her mouth. "Are you ok?", he asks as he holds her face. "I'm fine. Just going to take some getting use to." They walk out of the bathroom and into the den. His dad sits watching television. "Where's Adam?", asks Sean. "He went outside for a minute." Sean turns and walks to the door and opens it. Adam stands just outside gazing outward. Sean walks up beside of him. Lana follows. "What are you doing out here?", asks Sean.

"I'm wondering what mom is doing. If she knew anything that has happened in the past hours she would've flipped out. I hope she's ok." "Don't worry. I'm sure she's ok." Lana speaks. "I can tell you if she's ok." "How?", asks Adam. "I am a medium", she says with a smile. "Oh yeah. What color's my underwear?" "Blue", she says. "Holy shit", Adam says. "What am I thinking right now?" Sean steps in, "Enough Adam. No one cares what you are thinking." "Ok. Sorry. But tell me one thing, are we going to make it through this?" "You will have to chose at one point your life or your fathers." "What about me?", asks Sean. She turns to Sean and smiles. "I will always protect you. Nothing will ever happen to you." As Adam turns to walk inside he says, "This sucks. Why can't I find a cool girl?" "Come on. Let's go to bed", says Sean to Lana. They turn and open the door and walk inside. Sean closes the door behind him. They walk to Sean's room and shut the door. Sean pulls the cover back on the bed. "Sean. I don't sleep." "Your kidding." "No. I'll just keep watch over you." "Well, I'm tired." Sean climbs into bed and closes his eyes. She sits on the side and waits till he wakes up.

The next morning Sean wakes. He rises up in bed. Lana still sits in the same spot. "Good morning", she says. "Morning", says Sean. "Did you sleep well?" "Yeah. I didn't dream at all." Sean gets up out of bed and puts his clothes on. They both walk out of the room and into the kitchen where they are startled by visitors. It's the Reaper and the Shadow. "Hello Sean", the Reaper says. "Ready to go?" Sean looks over and see his dad and Adam lying on the sofa. "Oh don't worry about them. They're just asleep." "What do you want me to do?", asks Sean. "We have another planet to visit. Are you up for the challenge?" Sean thinks to himself, "I wonder what my reward is this time?" He looks at the Reaper and says, "Let's go, but she has to come, too." "Very well", the Reaper says. He opens up a portal as all four step in. The portal shuts.

On a small planet the portal opens. The Reaper steps out in human form. The others follow. Sean looks up toward the sky. Huge strange birds fly off in the distance. "So where are we?" "We are on a planet inhabited by forces of the unknown", says the Reaper. Lana stands by Sean's side closely clinching his arm. Weird sounds are heard off in the woods. "What the hell was that?", asks Sean. "That is why we are here", says the Reaper. "Don't worry Lana. I will protect you", says Sean. They begin walking in the direction of the noise. As they turn a corner they come upon little children eating some kind of animal. "Ok Sean. Now go kill them", the Reaper says. "They're just children. Why would I kill them?" "Take a closer look", says the Reaper as he pushes Sean toward them. This startles the children and sends them into a rage. They begin to change shape, turning into giants that are twenty feet tall. "Oh crap!", yells Sean. While they can't see anyone, but Sean, they charge toward him waving broken tree branches and blades. Sean falls to his feet while trying to run backwards. "Get up Sean!", Lana yells. He gets up and dodges the huge tree branches and blades while running through the crowd. He disappears from Lana's sight. All she can see is the backs of the giants. "Sean?", she says. The wind begins to blow. A huge lightning bolt parts the crowd knocking every giant down. Sean stands with his legs and arms apart with electricity running through his body. The light is so bright that everyone has to cover their eyes. The giants' bodies catch on fire. Lana has to cover her nose and mouth from the smell. One by one the giants turn to ash. Sean's light slowly goes out and he falls to the ground. Lana races over to him. "Sean!" She holds him in her arms. "I don't know if I can stand much more of this", he says. "Did I get them all?" "Yeah" She helps him up and wipes him off. The Reaper walks over to him. "Thank you Sean. You did a good job. When you get back to your family your reward will be there as well. Your Shadow will take you back now. Sean and Lana walk past the Reaper as he changes shape. They follow the Shadow into the portal. Sean looks back over his shoulder and watches the Reaper collect his souls. "Wait a second. The souls where really children?", he exclaims. The portal closes.

The portal reopens and Sean and Lana step out. The Shadow stays in as the portal closes and disappears. Sean looks around for his reward, but doesn't find anything. "Maybe it's in the cabin", she says. They walk up the steps and open the front door. As they walk in the place looks different inside. "Well there they are! Where have ya'll been?", his mom says. "Holy Shit!", says Sean. "Mom?" She walks over to him. "Now is that any way to great your mom?" "What are

you doing here?", he asks. "What do you mean silly? I live here."
Then his dad walks in from the back room. "Honey I need to go to the
store. Oh hey! We were wondering where you two went." "Um, dad",
says Sean with a suprise look on his face. "What son?" "Nevermind"
Sean takes Lana to his room. "Now don't you two be doing anything
in there you're not supposed to be doing", his dad says laughing.
Sean enters his room with Lana behind him and sit down on his bed.
"What the hell is going on? I'm not even sure we are on the same
planet. Why is my mom here? Even better, why is she talking to my
dad?" "This is your reward Sean", says Lana. "I never had parents.
You should be happy." I am happy, but it's just too weird." Lana lays
down behind Sean. "Lay with me", she says. Sean kicks his shoes off
and lays down facing her. "It's ok. I'm here and your mom and dad
are back together." "Where is Adam?", Sean asks. "Hey Adam!", he
yells, but there is no answer. He gets up out of bed and walks into the
den where his mom and dad are. "Have ya'll seen Adam?" "Who's
Adam?", his mom asks. "Yeah son?", asks his dad. "Nevermind", he
says. He turns around and runs back into his room. "Adam doesn't
exist!", he tells Lana. "I think the Reaper took him". "Well let's just
sleep on it and wait for the Reaper to come back", says Lana. He
lays back down beside her with his back toward her as she holds him
tight. He drifts off to sleep quickly.

The next morning Sean awakes. He gets up and puts new clothes
on. He looks over to find Lana still asleep. He smiles and walks out of
the room and into the kitchen. There he is met by his mom and dad
hanging all over each other. "Hey son" "Hey dad". "You want some
orange juice?" "Sure" His dad pours him some and just as Sean puts
it in his mouth his mother speaks. "Your father and I have some good
news to tell you. You're going to be a big brother!" Sean spits the juice
across the room. He wipes his mouth saying, "How is that possible? I
thought you two hated each other?" His dad looks at his mother. "Son
I've never hated your mother" "And I've never hated your father"
Sean begins to feel dizzy. "Are you ok son?", his dad asks. "I think I
better go lay down" He takes two steps and falls to the ground. His
body then catches on fire. "Oh my god! Sean!", his mom yells. "Don't
touch him", his dad yells. "Look. It's not burning his body." Lana comes
walking out of the room. "Sean!" She runs up to him and picks his

body up. She turns to ice as his flames go out. His parents watch in disbelief. She slowly puts him back down on the sofa. He opens his eyes. "What happened?", he asks. "You passed out and caught on fire" "You really scared us Sean. You two mind explaining to your mother and I what that was all about?" Sean looks at Lana. "He catches on fire sometimes" "Do we need to take you to a doctor?", his dad asks. "No. I'm fine" Sean rises up. "I just need some fresh air" He walks out the front door followed by Lana. "Sean wait up! I know all of this is weird right now, but trust me there is an explanation" "I just want to know where my brother is" She walks up to him and puts her arms around him. "Just wait till I see that Reaper again" "I would be careful what I say to him if I were you Sean" "It just pisses me off that I'm his little bitch" "He gave you me didn't he?" "Yeah. I guess he did" "Don't worry about your brother. He's ok. Now come on. Let's go back inside" "Alright" As they turn to go back inside, a portal opens up from behind. The Reaper steps out alone this time. Sean and Lana stop and turn around. "There you are. I've been waiting for you", says Sean. The Reaper points to the portal. "No no no. First you tell me where my brother is" Sean's mom and dad walk out of the front door. "Sean your father and I need to go get some groceries. We'll be back soon" Only Sean and Lana can see the Reaper. Sean looks at the Reaper. The Reaper points to Sean's mother. "What are you trying to say? What that my Adam is going to be my little brother. This makes no sinse" "Sean maybe we went back in time or something. Maybe you're Adam and Sean is your little brother, but your names are switched. I don't know" "Maybe the Reaper can explain it. Hey Reaper is she right?" The Reaper nods. "I don't understand why he would do this" The Reaper turns to human form as soon as Sean's parents leave. He walks up to Sean. "I did this, because I wanted to give you a fresh start. When your brother is born you will actually become him again, but you will remember everything. Use what you have learned wisely, but do not abuse it or I will take it back. Choose the right path and you will recieve rewards. The Reaper turns and walks back to the portal. "Are you two coming?", the Reaper asks. Sean holds Lana's hand as they walk into the portal. As the portal closes the Reaper turns back into himself.

"So where are we going this time?", asks Sean. The Reaper replies, "I want to show you something that is very interesting." The portal reopens to another strange land. They step out one by one. Sean looks around, but can only see desert. "There's nothing here", he says. "Wait for it", the Reaper says. Suddenly, a man appears from a distance running and stumbling. As Lana walks slowly up to Sean's side she asks, "Who is that?" The Reaper replies, "Jesus. We are still on Earth, but in the past obviously. "So what place is this?", asks Sean. "We are in the Judean desert", the Reaper says. "Can he see us?", asks Lana. "I don't know", the Reaper says. Sean starts to run up to Jesus when he is quickly stopped by some sort of demonic creature. It turns to Sean and hisses at him. Then it turns around and takes off running toward Jesus. It morphs into a human just before it reaches him. "Come back Sean", yells Lana. Sean turns around and runs back to her. "I don't understand. Why are you showing me this?", asks Sean to the Reaper. The Reaper looks back and says, "try to think outside the box". Sean can do nothing but watch. "What is he trying to give Jesus?", asks Sean. "It doesn't matter. He will not take it", says the Reaper. Then the demonic creature disappears. "Where'd he go?", asks Lana. Time speeds up as darkness falls. They stand and watch Jesus stagger. He falls to his feet as a bright light shines above him. He looks up slowly and smiles. Beautiful angels flow downward all around him. He looks around at all of them. One walks up to him with a bag of water. Another walks up to him with bread. One after another, each angel walks up to him with some type of nourishment. "Thank you. Oh thank you", he says. The Reaper turns around and walks back to the portal. "Let's move on shall we", he says. Sean and Lana turn around as well and walk back to the portal. The portal closes and vanishes.

The portal reopens quickly to a planet that is dark and filled with volcanic activity all around. "Watch your step", says the Reaper. Only small pieces of land still exist. Sean and Lana jump across the small pieces as the Reaper glides across. "There can't possibly be anything left alive on this planet", says Sean. "There's nothing but demons here", says the Reaper. Thousands of demons come from everywhere. "We're surrounded!", yells Sean. He fires his lightning up and waves it toward the demons. It knocks them down, but only stuns them. "Lana! Help me!" Lana runs over to the edge of a lava pit. She turns her arms to ice and forces them into the lava. Steam flows as she yells out in pain. "Ah!" Sean keeps the demons back by smacking them with lightning bolts. Lana's ice begins to freeze the entire planet. The ice covers it in a matter of seconds. All of the surrounding demons become ice. Sean clinches his fist as tight as he can to build up a super bolt! As he explodes with electricity, so do the frozen demons. Sean's body is ripped apart for a matter of seconds, but then comes right back to where it was. He falls to one knee with a bloody nose. Lana runs up to him. "Are you ok?" "Yeah", he whispers. "I've never seen you do that." "I didn't know I could do that." He rises to his feet. "There all yours", he says to the Reaper. The Reaper wastes no time and starts collecting. "I don't get it though. What does he want with demon souls?", asks Sean. "Maybe they are trapped souls", she says. They stand back and watch patently. After the Reaper is done he reopens the portal and they step in. It closes and reopens in Sean's room back at his mom's house. Sean and Lana step out, but the Reaper stays in. "I might be back for you Sean", says the Reaper. "I hope not", says Sean. Just as the portal closes there is a knock on the door. "Knock knock." "Come in", says Sean. The door opens and it's his mom. "Hey hun, you and Lana want something to eat or drink?" "Sure mom." Lana and Sean follow his mom into the kitchen. His dad sits in a chair at the table eating some food, but Sean can't quite make out what it is. His dad keeps shoveling it in his mouth and eating like a pig. "Now you two sit right down. I've fixed something wonderful to eat. Sean sits in a chair right across from Lana. "Um mom." "Yes dear." "Where's Adam?" His mom giggles, "He's right here", she says as she puts a plate in the center of the table with Adam's severed head on it. "Dig in!"

# CHAPTER III

Sean screams out loud, "Ah!" His heart races as he panics and rises to his feet. He runs half way around the table and grabs Lana'a hand. She gets up and runs with him to his room. As he enters his room he can hear his mother shout in the back ground, "I thought you liked meat?" Sean slams the door behind him. Another portal stands open. Sean looks at Lana and says, "Come on". They jump into the portal and it closes. They fall through space until the portal reopens above a lake. Sean and Lana are spit out into the water. They franticly swim towards a small dock and pull themselves up. Sean climbs out first and then pulls lana out. "Are you ok?", he asks. "I'm fine", she says. They take a moment to catch their breath. Lana looks at Sean and asks, "Do you think your parents really killed Adam?" Sean thinks back to Adams head on a platter. "No. I don't. I think that was just some weird parallel universe or something." He looks around and sees something familiar. His dad's cabin sits up on a hill not too far away. "Come on", he says. They start walking off the dock and through some tall grass. A noise is heard from behind. They stop walking and turn around. Another portal opens and four demon dogs run out. "What the hell are those?", asks Sean. "Shock them!", she yells. Sean raises his arms, but just as he does he is attacked by the dogs, knocking him to the ground. Lana jumps on one of the dogs as it bucks like a horse. She turns to ice and bear hugs it. As the dog turns into a solid piece of ice she smashes it to pieces. Sean grabs their heads and electrifies them causing them to explode at the same time and sending brain matter all over. The third dog runs back into the portal as it closes behind him. Sean and Lana are left sitting on the ground covered in dead dog. He looks over to her and says, "When I see the Reaper again I'm gonna kick his ass, because I know he sent those damn things just to test me." Lana stands up and helps him up, while brushing him off. "Let's get to the cabin", he says. As they reach the cabin they walk up the front steps. Sean peeks through the windows. "I don't see anyone". A face appears suddenly scaring the crap out of Sean. "Ah!" He backs off quickly almost falling to the floor. "Go away!", a deep voice yells. "I'm looking for my dad", says Sean. "I said go away!" The whole front part of the cabin is blasted apart from the inside. Sean and Lana fly through the air backwards landing on their backs. After the debri clears the man walks out from what used to be the front door. "I thought I told you to go away. Now I have to rebuild my cabin", the old man says. "Sean?", the old man asks with complete suprise. "Dad?", says Sean as he stands up. "Is that really you dad?" They walk slowly toward each other. His dad asks with tears in his eyes, "Where have you been all this time? You haven't gotten any older either." "I can't explain it dad. Where's mom?" "She died years ago. She was in a car wreck while she and I were going to the store. I broke my leg, but that was all." "Did you see the Reaper dad?" His dad drifts off staring at the ground. "Dad!", shouts Sean. His dad looks up and says, "You two should go. It's not safe for you to be here." He waves his hand and a portal opens behind Sean and Lana. "How did you do that?", asks Sean. "Something happened to me the first time I saw the Reaper. That day I ran the red light, as I passed in and out the Reaper got closer and closer to me. He went right through me. Every since then I think he left me these powers." He looks down at his hands and clinches them shut. "Go now" "But dad" "I said go. You don't belong here" Sean takes Lana's hand, turns around and walks into the portal. The portal closes before they can even turn around. Lana grips Sean's hand as they fly through space and time. Sean wonders to himself where the portal is going to spit them out this time. A figure flys by going the opposite direction. Sean looks back at it. The figure is the Reaper. It looks back at them, but keeps going.

The portal opens up in front of Sean's mom's house. As they step out, Lana asks, "Where are we?" Sean replies, "My mom's house. Come on." They walk up the driveway and up to the front door. Sean grabs the knob and turns it slowly. He opens the door and walks in with Lana right on his heels. As he looks around the room, he sees his mother lying on the couch. He walks over to her and kneels down. "Mom" She opens her eyes and smiles. "Sean!", she says as she raises up and hugs him. "Where have you been? Your father and I have been looking for you for days" She starts crying so Sean comforts her in his arms. "It's ok mom. I'm here" "I'm sorry. I'm just a little emotional after all that's been happening. First you go missing then your brother" "Wait a minute. Adam's missing?" "When you disappeared Adam took off after you. He just never came back", she says with tears in her eyes. Sean stands up and says, "Don't worry mom. I'm gonna find him. You just get some rest." She lays back down exhausted from all her worrying. "By the way, this is my girl friend Lana." His mother doesn't reply. "Come on Sean", Lana says. They walk back out of the house. Sean walks down the steps and onto the front lawn where he falls to his knees. He looks to the sky and yells out, "Why are you doing this to me and my family God?" Lana walks up behind him, "God doesn't interfer with you or your families lives. The Reaper on the otherhand can." "You don't think the Reaper has Adam do you?", asks Sean as he turns around. "If he does it means he's dead." Sean's stomach growls. "I'm hungry. Let's go back inside and eat." They walk back into the house and into the kitchen. Sean walks over to the frig and opens it. He pulls out some lunch meat to make him and Lana a sandwich. He also grabs a jar of mayo and a loaf of bread sitting on the counter. He then puts everything on the table and begins making the sandwiches. "I don't want one", she says while staring at the food. "I can make you something else if you like" "I'll just eat later", she says. "Okay", he says. He grabs the sandwich and they go to his room. His sits on his bed as Lana crawls up behind him. He turns on his t.v. that only has about three channels. "Nothing but the news on. I hate t.v. during the day", he says with disappointment. The news anchor speaks, "Today a young male's body was found today in the woods from what appears to be a self-inflicted gun shot wound to the head. Unfortunately, the male cannot be identified yet" Sean turns the t.v. off with a blank look on his face. "We need to find that boy's body before mom and dad do".

Sean walks out of his room with Lana. "Mom. Can I borrow your car?" "Sure honey", she mumbles. He grabs her keys off the kitchen table and walks out the front door. Walking to the car, sean sees the next door neighbor standing on her front porch smoking. She waves and smiles with rotten teeth. Sean pays her no mind as she starts coughing. He walks up to Lana's door and lets her in. She hops in and he closes the door. He runs around to the driver's side and opens the door. He gets in, but just as he closes it the neighbor pops up on Lana's side. Sean and Lana both scream, "Ah!" "What the hell lady?", says Sean. The lady smiles and says, "I thought you were dead. Mmm. You smell like cookies little girl." She leans in the car and licks Lana's face. "Ah! Get away from me", screams Lana. The ladies eyes turn black as she smiles and laughs. Sean stretches his arm out in front of Lana and electrifies the woman sending her flying back into her own yard. She lays on the ground twitching. "Wait in the car", says Sean as he opens his door and gets out. He walks over to the lady as she lays on her back with her eyes closed. Smoke rises from her hair and clothes. Sean covers his nose as he walks up closely. "Is she dead?", asks Lana. He looks over at Lana. "Yeah. I fried her good" The lady opens her eyes and screams, "Ahhh!" She vanishes and reappears on here front porch looking like she was never burnt. She sticks another cigarette in her mouth and strikes a match. She lights the cigarette and shakes the match out. Then she nonchalantly stands and stares at Sean. "How you doing Sean?", she asks. He stands breathing heavily and confused. He then runs back to the car and gets in. He slams the door as Lana asks, "Are you okay? Why are you sweating so much?" He looks at her and asks, "Please tell me that you saw that, too." "I'm not sure I follow", she says. "You didn't just see what that crazy old woman did?" "Sean you're scaring me" "Nevermind", he says as he puts the car in reverse and backs out of the driveway. As he puts the car into drive, he looks over to see the old woman gone. He drives off and looks back in the rear view mirror. The demon-like old woman floats up behind the car quickly, but Sean closes his eyes as tight as he can and then reopens them after a moment. He turns around and looks out the back window, but there is no one there. He turns back around and continues driving when Lana asks, "Are you ok?" "I'm fine", he says.

They arrive at the hospital to hopefully locate the unidentified body. As they walk through the front door they are greeted by a lady sitting behind a desk. Lana hangs back as Sean asks the lady, "Can you help me? I'm trying to locate the unidentified body that possibly came in earlier." "Yes. If you just go down this hall to your left and then to your right you will see a man at another desk. He will help you." "Thank you", he replies. "Come on", he says to Lana. She follows him, but not to quickly or closely. They walk down a hallway just like the lady said and then turn to the right. A man sits behind a small desk on the left just before a set of double doors. "Hello. I'm here to see the unidentified body that just came in." "The man looks up from his newspaper. "Sign here", he says pointing to a sheet of paper. Sean picks up a pen and signs his name as well as Lana's. "Follow me please", the man says. He walks through the double doors as Sean and Lana follow. The man walks over to a row of cabinets and opens a door. He slides the body out, which lays on a long platform. The body is covered in a white sheet. Just before the man removes the sheet he says, "I will fore worn you it's not a pretty sight". He pauses and then pulls back the sheet exposing the halfway blown apart head. Lana looks away quickly, but Sean looks at it closely. "Do you know this person?", asks the man. Sean begins to tear up. He slowly backs up as his face turns red from anger. "Hey are you ok?", the man asks. Sean yells out as he burst into flames, "No!" Lana stands back and does nothing. The room gets so hot it melts everyhthing in sight including the man. Lana turns to ice and slowly walks up to Sean putting her arms around him. Steam fills the room as Sean is extinguished. The Reaper appears across the room. Sean and Lana look up at it. It opens it robe as the soul of the man walks into it. Sean shouts, "Where's my brother you son of a bitch?", as he runs toward the Reaper. The Reaper closes its robe and begins to disappear as Sean makes a fist and lunges toward him. He ends up punching through then air and landing face first on the ground. Lana rushes over to help him up. She puts his arm around her shoulder and says, "Come on. We've got to get out of here." They run to the way they came in, but just before they walk out, Lana puts her hand on the wall. The ice from here fingertips flows throughout the room covering the walls, ceiling and floor. When she lets go the room is one big hollow block of ice. They walk out of the room calmly as hospital staff run past them. They make it outside and walk to the car. She helps him into the passenger side and shuts his door. She then runs around to the driver's side and opens the door and gets in. "Give me your keys", she says. He pulls them out of his pocket and hands them to her. She puts the key in the ignition and starts the car. "Do you know what you're doing?", he asks. "I watched you do it. How hard can it be?", she says. He reaches over his shoulder and puts his seat belt on. She puts hers on as well. She puts the car in reverse and backs out of the parking place. She rams another parked car. "Oops!" She then puts the car in drive and floors it. "Woohoo!", she shouts. Sean grabs onto his seat belt for dear life. The car flies out of the parking lot and out into the road. As the car turns right, she smokes the right rear tire.

A mile or so down the road, Sean asks Lana, "Could you please slow down just a little bit. I don't feel so good." "Oh, sorry." She lets up a little and asks, "So where should we go now?" Sean looks at her and says, "Home". "What are you going to tell your parents?" "Nothing". "Why not?" "What would you say? What that I found Adam and oh yeah he blew his head off, but unfortunately you can't go see his body, because I torched it." "I guess you have a point" "Look maybe there's another way to fix this like finding the Reaper and making him open another portal to the past or something" "I don't know Sean. Once the Reaper has a soul he's not letting it go." "I'll just have to be more convincing I guess."

The car pulls into the drive at Sean's mom's house. He opens the door and gets out, but not before looking over at the neighbors house. The house looks bare with no one home. Lana opens her door and gets out as well. They both walk up to his mom's house and go through the front door. "Let's go to my room. I need to think", replies Sean. They walk out of the kitchen, down the hall and into Sean's room. He closes the door behind them and then walks over and lays on the bed. She crawls up on top of him and rests her chin on his chest. "What are you thinking right now?", she asks. "I'm losing my mind", he replies. With a strange look on her face, Lana moves her head upward. "Are you ok?", asks Sean. Lana's long hair raises up as the static electricity takes hold. The room begins to light up with electricity. She tries covering her eyes by using Sean's chest. He puts his arms around her and turns his head away as well. The light is so bright it burns shadows into the wall. Sean and Lana together raise off the bed. The tenticles of the electricity curl around the room, but are then sucked back into the center of the room to form a small sphere the size of a softball. It floats in mid air and turns slowly. They turn their heads and stare at it not realizing that they are still floating about a foot above the bed. Everything in the room becomes weightless. Small objects float past their heads and that's when they realize something's wrong. Lana lets go of Sean and floats backwards. She smiles and giggles as she performs a back flip. They both float around the room together. "This is amazing!", says Sean. The sphere begins to pulsate and enlarges to the size of a basketball. "Sean. Did you see that?" "See what?" "The sphere got bigger." Sean looks at it. "Holy crap! It did get bigger!" "Sean. What if it keeps growing?" The sphere pulsates again and enlarges to the size of a beach ball. As Sean and Lana back up, Lana hides behind him. "What are we going to do?", she asks. Sean takes a deep breath and says, "I need you to stand back". Lana plants herself in a corner and tries not to move. Sean raises his arms and lets the electricity flow from them. The sphere increases its size about as big as Sean. It pulls the electricity from Sean and feeds off of his energy. His nose bleeds and his teeth grind. Not giving in, he fights the pain and clinches his fist. The room gains its gravity and Sean falls to his knees. Lana cowards in the corner as the sphere takes the tears from her eyes. The sphere takes on so much energy that it expands as large as the room. Lana and Sean are not killed, but are consumed instead. As he lowers his arms, Lana runs over to him. His head hangs as she cries out, "Sean!" She supports his head and watches his eyes roll back. Lana turns her hand to ice and touches his face. His skin freezes instantly. Before it consumes his entire face she lets go. A few seconds go by, but it is useless. She thinks fast and with super human strength she picks him up in her arms and carries him out of his room and out of the house. She then lays him out on the front lawn facing up. She looks up to the sky and says, "Fix him. I'm doing what I'm told so fix him" She looks back down at him and watches the sunlight brighten his face. The ice melts as he moves his head around. He moans and opens his eyes slowly. "Where am I?", he asks. "It's ok Sean. You're ok." She reaches down and lifts him up. He stands, but is still very weak. "What happened?", he asks. "I had to get you away from that sphere. It was draining away all your energy." "What about you? Did it do anything to you?" "It actually made me stronger", she says with a smile. Sounds of cracking come from the house. "Mom!", he yells. He tries to run up the front steps and open the door, but is too late. The house crumbles leaving the giant sphere. Sean walks backwards and bumps into what he thinks is Lana. He turns around to see the Reaper staring right at him. Sean turns to his side, because he knows why the Reaper is there. It walks past him and straight into the house. It stops in the den and opens its robe. Sean's mom rises off the sofa and walks into the Reaper. Sean stands back and cries knowing he can do nothing. The Reaper then glides out of the house and past Sean. "Aren't you gonna do anything about the sphere?", asks Sean. The Reaper stops and turns around. He then holds his arm out and points two fingers at them. Sean looks at Lana and then back at the Reaper. "I don't understand", says Sean. "Sean I think he means we have to destroy it together" The Reaper lowers his arm as a portal opens up behind him. He floats backwards into the portal and it slowly closes. Sean and Lana are left behind to decide what to do.

"I have an idea", says Lana. She gets behind Sean as they both face the giant sphere. She reaches around him and grabs both of his arms. "I'm going to freeze your arms and hands. When I do you shock the hell out of the sphere", she says. She turns his arms and hands to ice. Sean begins to steam up. The electricity flows through his arms while the ice stays in tact. He blasts the sphere with more power than ever before. "It feels weird!", he shouts. "Keep going!', she replies. Instead of electricity going everywhere, it instead comes out of him in one solid stream. The sphere starts to turn black and krinkles under preasure. It loses it negative gravity and falls to the ground. Sean stops and Lana lets go. Instead of falling to the ground, Sean stands with his arms to his side breathing heavily. The ice on his arms disappears. Lana stands behind him breathing heavily as well. Sean turns around and says, "That was unlike the other times before. How did you know that would work?" "I didn't", she says. They walk over to the sphere. "Wonder what it is?", she asks. "It ain't from this world", he says. Sean walks closer to it and puts his hand on it. "Its vibrating!", he says. Lana walks closer to it and touches it as well. "I thought we killed it, but apparently we just put it in some kind of cacoon." "Great", says Sean. "We can't just leave it here. We need to destroy it." "I need to absorb its energy", she says. She turns her whole body to ice. "You better stand back Sean" He turns and runs to the front lawn. Lana makes a fist and punches through the sphere. The light from it shines brightly through her. As she takes most of the sphere's energy she cries out, "Ah!" "Are you ok?", asks Sean. She doesn't answer. She breathes intensly and with every breath she takes is one step closer to extacy. The ground shakes while Sean tries to keep his balance. The ground breaks up and he falls to the ground. Giant oak trees fall all around. She pulls her hand out of the sphere and screams so loud Sean has to cover his ears. "Ah!" The sphere explodes into tiny pieces. Everything it touches burns like acid. Some of it lands on Sean and catches his clothes on fire. He slaps it out quickly before it spreads. After the earth quake has stopped, Sean climbs to his feet and looks around. Everything is destroyed. He then looks over at Lana. She stands naked and her body is ice. "Are you ok?", asks Sean. She turns around and her eyes glow blue. She doesn't say anything though. She just walks toward Sean and stops right in front of him. "Are you ok?", he asks again. She nods, but that is all. Sean knows something is not right with her so he just plays dumb for right now. "We need to get out of here before the cops get here", he says. He grabs her hand and runs up the front steps with her and to where his room use to be. "Here. Put these on", he says while handing here a pair of jeans and a t-shirt. "Here is a pair of my shoes, too." With a calm look on her face, she takes all of it and puts it on. Sirens are heard from about a mile away. "We need to go now", he says. They run out the front and down the street. "I know where we can go for right now", says Sean. They walk for about a mile and come upon the poolhall where Sean first had his accident. "Let's go around the back" Sean leads the way to the back alley. Her face begins to melt. Sean looks back at her. "Good. I didn't think you were ever going to melt" As Sean turns back around he bumps into a man. "Give me you wallet!", the man shouts. Sean backs up protecting Lana. "I don't have any money and neither does she" "Well then", the nasty man says with a green grin. "Good day to you miss", he says bowing over. "Aren't you a pretty little thing" He walks over to her, but doesn't get close. Sean steps in. "If you touch her I will kill you" "Oh yeah and how are you going to do that?", the man says laughing. Sean grabs the man's chest and shocks him with more power than a cattle prod. He shakes and is thrown backwards up against a wall. He lands in some garbage and almost passes out. Sean walks over to him and leans over, "You know there's a reason why you live this way. Maybe you should find out what that reason is and fix it" Sean and Lana walk away as the man is left sitting in the trash. "There's two entrances to this place. We'll go in the back door" They get to the end of the alley when everything comes back to Sean slowly. He stops and Lana asks him, "What's wrong?" He looks to the ground and says, "This is where I hit my head" "Come on Sean. I want to go inside", she says while grabing his arm. She pulls him away as they walk out of the alley and to the back door. She is gitty with excitment. Sean reaches for the knob and opens the door for her. She walks in and he follows. Inside, people are sitting at the bar drinking and chatting and the pool tables are filled except for one in the back. "Let's grab the table in the back", he says. "We need to be seen by these people in here so we can't be placed at my house for what happened" "What is this game called?", she asks. "Pool", he says. About ten minutes go by when two police officers walk in. Sean looks up from a shot, "Oh crap". "Just relax", she says. They mean us no harm. The bartender leaves with the officers. "Wonder what that was all about?", asks Sean. A couple of hours pass and Sean and Lana leave the poolhall. "Where should we go now?", she asks. Sean looks forward, "With him". "Huh?", lana asks. The Reaper stands in front of them across the street waiting patiently beside a portal. Sean whispers, "When's it gonna end?" Lana grabs his hand. "Wherever you go I go". They walk to the Reaper and start to cross the street, but just as they do a truck hits both of them.

"Sean! Can you hear me?", a voice asks. Sean, looking up at the sealing of a vehicle, flashes in and out. "Sean! You're gonna be ok", a man says. He puts an oxygen mask over Sean's face. The ambulance races down the road in and out of traffic. "Come on Sean stay with me" Sean looks over to his right and see Lana sitting and smiling. "You're going to be ok Sean", she says. Sean passes out.

"Sean. Sean can you hear me?" He opens his eyes slowly and sees Lana standing on his left. "There you are. I was beginning to worry for a moment there. How are you feeling?" "Ok I guess" "Well, don't you worry. I'm right here and I'm not going to let anything happen to you" "What happened?", he asks. "You poor thing. You don't remember anything do you? I was told that you had some kind of seizure or something. You fell and hit your cute little head", she says smiling. "You seem different", he says. "What do you mean? This is the first time you've seen me silly. I tell you what. You just sit tight and I'll bring you some icecream" As she leaves the room, he begins to panic. He tries to move, but he can't because his legs are asleep. He closes his eyes and calms himself. He raises his hand toward the ceiling and flicks his wrist, but nothing happens. He then tries his other hand, but still nothing happens. Lana walks back in with the icecream on a plate and sits it on a stand next to the bed. "Well, I see your arms are working. Maybe we'll get those legs aworkin, too" She pulls up a chair and sits down beside him. "I'm so glad I get to feed you now. Eating through a tube just doesn't cut it" She puts a napkin under his chin and then grabs a spoon and begins feeding him. "Mmm", now isn't that good?" Sean gulps every bite with a smile. Before he knows it the icecream is gone. "All gone", she says. "Now you just rest", she says. She starts to turn away when he says, "I wanna walk". She looks at him and smiles, "Ok".

In another room, Sean struggle to walk, while Lana stands behind supporting him. "Come on Sean. You can do it. Just one foot at a time" An hour goes by. "Sean I think you should rest" "I don't want to rest!", he shouts. "I need to keep going" "Alright then", she says. Several hours pass by and Sean finally stops. "I've never seen anyone as strong as you Sean", she says, while sitting and watching him walk on his hands. "I've never seen anyone recover as fast as you either" Sean sits on the floor and stares at Lana. "What?", she asks. "Who are you really?", he asks. "I've been trying to find that out my whole life", she says looking away and smiling. "What really happened to me?" She looks back at him. "I'm not suppose to talk about it"

"Sean walks over to her on his knees. "Please tell me. I need to know. I promise I won't tell anyone" She looks to her right, "The night they brought you in I thought you were dead. Your head was split open. There was blood everywhere. The doctors worked on you all night. When they were done you were in a coma. I was asigned to you and I've been here ever since" "Wait a minute. This doesn't make since. I came out of the coma months ago" "Sean you have been in the coma for over a year now. In fact, you're still in one now"

Sean awakens lying in his bed in a motel room to find himself lying next to Lana. He rubs his face, because he is not sure if this is real or not. "Lana", he says. "Mmm", she replies. He jumps out of bed and looks out the window. Birds play and sing in the trees. He walks over and turns the t.v. on. and sits back down on the bed. "Nothing but the news on again", he says. "Come back to bed baby" "Hang on", he says. The news reporter says, "Today a house is left in ruins and a small neighborhood as well. An Earthquake appears to have struck, but only demolishes one house" "Yes!", Sean shouts. "They think it was an Earthquake. Ha ha idiots", he says as he shuts the t.v. off. He jumps back in bed with Lana. "Mmm", she says. "It's too early Sean" "Come on Lana. Get up. Let's get out of here" "Where are we supposed to go?" "I don't know. We can hitch a ride up to the mountains" "I don't feel good", she says as she gets out of bed and runs to the bathroom. "Blah!" She throws up in the toilet. "Are you ok sweetie?" "I'm fine. I just need to eat that's all" She wipes her mouth and climbs over to the sink. She turns on the cold water and splashes it on her face. She then grabs a wash cloth and wipes her face. She then walks out of the bathroom and puts her jeans on and t-shirt. Sean puts his shirt and jeans on as well. "There's a small cafe around the corner. We can get something to eat there", says Sean. As they walk out of the motel, Sean is met by his dad. "Dad. How did you know I was here?" His dad looking suspicious quickly replies, "I was looking for your brother. I've been looking for you both actually". He walks up to Sean and puts his arms around him. "Where have you been boy?" "It's a long story", replies Sean. "Sean we need to go", says Lana. "Dad I need to go, but I will be home soon. I just need to take care of some stuff" "Ok", his dad replies. Just as Sean walks away, a woman steps out from one of the rooms. "Hurry back ok. I'm getting cold". Sean's dad turns around and says, "Ok".

Sean walks beside Lana to the cafe just around the corner. "How did your dad find you?" "I don't think he was looking for me" "What makes you say that?" "My dad doesn't know how smart I am. I know why he was at the motel. My parents have never given me any credit for being smart" "So why was he at the motel?" Sean stops walking and turns to Lana. "He was there with another woman" He turns and keeps walking. Lana follows. "How do you know this?" "I smelled the perfume on him when he hugged me. Mom doesn't wear perfume. She's alergic" They arrive at the cafe and walk through the front door. The room is filled full of people. "Over there", he says pointing to a booth to the left. They walk over and sit down. A waitress walks over. "Hey can I help ya'll?" "I'll have a water", Lana says. "And for you sir?" "I'll have milk please" "Give us a few minutes to decide", says Sean. "Ok", says the waitress. She walks away. Sean looks around the room at all the people. "Would you relax. You're making me nervous", Lana says. "Do you ever feel like you're being watched?", he asks. "No", she says. "Well right now I feel that way" "Look just try to relax" The waitress comes back with their drinks. "Have ya'll decided?" "I'll have a steak rare", says Lana. "I'll have bacon and eggs", he says. "Ok. Coming right up" The waitress walks away. "That's kind of unusal to eat in the morning", says Sean. "Sean I think there's something wrong with me. I think I might be pregnant" He just about knocks his milk over. "Are you sure? I mean, have you taken a test?" "What you don't want to have a kid with me?", she says with anger. "No. It's not that. I just want to be sure that you're ok" "I'm fine", she says. She leans back and crosses her arms. The arm on the clock on the wall begins to slow until it finally stops. Sean looks around the room and then at Lana. Everyone including her is frozen in time. The front door flies open with a burst of wind. The Reaper walks in with the Shadow trailing behind. The Reaper morphs into human form as he walks up to Sean. He leans down to Sean and asks, "Have you been a naughty little boy Sean?" "I don't know what you mean", says Sean. "Don't play innocent with me", the Reaper says as he raises back up. "I've come to help you Sean. I want the child. I can make all this go away if you let me. Just walk the other way" Sean gets up from his seat and walks past the Reaper. "The Shadow will take care of you" Sean doesn't think twice. He walks out of the cafe with the Shadow. He opens up a portal and they both disappear in seconds. The Reaper takes the soul from the child and disappears as well.

"Where do you want to go Sean?", asks the Shadow. "I don't know", he replies. "I can take you anywhere at any point in time" "I want to see if I can stop my brother from killing himself. Take me there" "Ok, but I don't think you're going to like what you're going to see" "Just take me" The Shadow guides them through an obsticle course of worm holes with his hand. The portal opens in the middle of a forest. Sean and the Shadow step out as the portal closes. "Where's he at? I don't see him" "Just wait" Adam comes almost out of nowhere running as fast as he can. He trips and falls to the ground. He tries to get up, but just before he can his dad comes from behind and knocks him out with a knock to the head from a large pistol. Sean thinks fast and runs up to him. He kicks the gun from his hand, but his dad backhands him knocking him to the ground. "Ah!" His dad walks over and picks up the gun. He pulls back the trigger and points it at Sean. His dad can't believe his eyes. "Sean? Is that you?" Sean picks himself off the ground rubbing his face. "What are you trying to do dad?" "When you went missing he went crazy and tried to kill your mother and I. I have to put him down before he hurts someone" "No dad. There's a better way. I'll take him away with me. Sean puts his hands out in front of him and walks slowly over to Adam. He kneels down and tries to wake Adam. "Adam wake up" He slaps him across his face. Adam wakens and climbs to his feet. "Sean. You're alive!", he says hugging him. "Adam calm down. I'm gonna take you away with me" Adam turns around to see his dad standing there with a gun behind his back. His dad smiles and says, "That right Adam. Sean's gonna take good care of you" "Come on Adam", says Sean as he puts his arm around him. They walk into the woods as their dad turns around and walks the other way. As soon as their dad is out of sight Sean stops walking. "Ok. I need to show you something, but you have to promise that you're not going to freak out on me", he says. "This is my friend the Shadow" The Shadow walks out from a bush. Adam jumps back in fear. "Ah! What the hell is that?" "Don't be afraid.

He's here to help" "How can he see me Sean?" Sean replies, "He's different that's all. Can he come with us?" "I suppose", the Shadow says. He opens up a portal. Adam can't believe his eyes. "Where are we going?", he asks. "Wherever you want", says Sean. Adam walks up to the portal and Sean follows. The Shadow steps in last. "So what is this thing?" "Its a transporter", the Shadow replies. It closes and they are sucked into outer space.

On another planet quite like Earth, the portal opens in the middle of a field where a great battle is just about to take place. The Shadow is the first to exit the portal. He turns around to Sean and Adam. "We must proceed with caution. There are many things here that won't hesitate to kill you". He turns back around and begins to walk forward. They follow him and slowly walk around to the side of him. Sean looks down, "My clothes have changed". "So have mine", says Adam. They are both wearing armor from a midevil time. "The portal does that sometimes. This way fitting in is easier", the Shadow says. "Fitting in for what?", asks Adam. A large crowd appears from the right and left. "Oh great!", says Sean with sarcasim. Adam is with nothing, but smiles. "You will find on your back a sword and on your side is a sawed off shot gun. There is a knife on the side of your boot as well", the Shadow says waving his hand to Adam. "What about me?", asks Sean. "Really?", asks the Shadow. "Oh yeah", says Sean. The Shadow holds his arms out in front of Sean and Adam with his back to them. "We wait until the battle begins then we strike", he says. "By the way Adam, your gun will never run out of ammunition" "Cool", says Adam. "Oh and I forgot to mention that you're not the only one that has a special power here Sean", says the Shadow. Adam looks over to Sean. "What does he mean by powers?" Sean looks back at him and smiles saying, "You'll see." He looks back at the Shadow and asks, "Which side are we on?" "Neither", the Shadow says. A loud horn sounds and both sides run towards one another screaming. "Ah!" Another portal opens across the field and the Reaper steps out. "Look!", says Sean pointing to the Reaper. "He will definately profit from this", says the Shadow. Creatures from both sides shoot flames from their hands at one another as well as electricity. Many are hit and killed, but the Reaper doesn't budge. Arrows are shot up in the air and great bolders are thrown from giants. The crowds clash with swords flying. "Ok. Get ready!", says the Shadow. "Now!" Sean and Adam take off running. The Shadow stays right in the middle of them mimicing Sean's every move. All of the weight that Adam had lost in the past suddenly comes back to him, but this time it increases his strenght. He is even able to run faster. Sean shocks everyone he can knocking creatures down left and right. A creature wearing a suit of armor and the head of a white wolf stands in one place shocking everything that gets near it. Sean stops and stares. "Sean! What are you crazy? Keeping fighting!", yells Adam. A man with a bear head lunges at Adam, but Adam gets the drop on him as he pulls his gun out and shoots him. "Boom!" One shot and the Bear man is sent flying backwards. Sean, captivated by the wolf, walks up to it lowering his arms. The wolf looks at Sean with anger in its eyes. It turns to light him up, but just before it can Adam comes out of nowhere and tackles the wolf knocking it out cold. As Adam climbs off of it, a sword is pushed through his chest from behind. "Adam!", shouts Sean as he runs over to his aid. Adam's body returns to its normal size as he lay in a pool of blood. This enfuriates Sean. He slowly stands up and runs to the thing that just killed his brother. A giant turns and runs for his life into the woods. Sean follows. For a second, Sean loses it. As he rounds a corner he hears a small child crying behind a tree. He walks up to the tree and finds a small boy crouched in a small ball covering his head with his arms and crying. "What are you doing here?", Sean asks. The boy looks up and asks, "Please don't kill me". "I'm not going to", says Sean. "Give me your hand". The boy reaches out for his hand and grabs it. Sean helps him stand, but just as he does the boy begins to laugh. "Ah ah ah" He quickly grows into a giant and slings Sean about twenty feet. Sean lands on his back. The giant walks over to him with a raised sword. He strikes at Sean, but Sean dives to the side. The giant picks the sword up and swings it sideways at Sean, but gets it stuck in a tree. Sean grabs the sword and sends electricity through it shocking the giant and setting him on fire. Sean then lets go and the giant does as well trying to put his flames out, but it is useless. He falls to the ground like a dead tree at Sean's feet. Sean takes the sword out of the tree and holds it up in front of him. He sends electricity through it as it glows a bright blue. He walks out of the forest with no much of a battle going on. Adam runs up to him. "There you are. What did you do? Did you have to take a piss or something?" "You're alive!", says Sean while hugging him. "Yeah. Thanks to your friend. He resurected me", he says pointing to the Shadow. The Shadow walks up. "Thank you", says Sean. "We have a battle to finish", the Shadow says. All three run into the crowd. Adam takes his sword out and cuts off heads. Sean swings his sword as well slicing up victims left and right. The creature with the wolf head appears in front of Sean once more with sword in hand. It charges him and Sean does the same. Their swords meet with great force as both of them equal each other in strenght. Sean grits his teeth, but loses his balance in the mud and slips and falls on his back. The wolf kicks Sean's glowing sword away from him. The wolf then lowers its sword and reaches up and takes its wolf mask off. Sean can't believe his eyes. A beautiful girl stands staring down at him. She throws her sword down. Adam can be seen in th back ground flying through the air like a sumo wrestler knocking down creatures as if they were bowling pins. The shadow can be seen as well levitating creatures and throwing them. "Who are you?", asks the girl. Sean gets up off the ground. "They call me the Lightning Rod", he says. "I'm White Lightning", she says. Sean looks around, "Tell you what, if you let me take you on a date I'll help you kill the bad guys", he says to her. "I don't know what a date is, but you have a deal". She turns around with Sean by her side. They both raise their arms as lightning feels the air. Electricity flows through them as they shock everyone with metal armor on. As they join hands, Sean turns to a dark blue flame. She turns into a light blue flame. Their power is unstopable. Everything in sight is burned up to a crisp. When it is all over Adam waits on the side with Shadow, while Sean and the girl walk over to them. The Reaper walks into the middle of the field and opens his robe. All the souls walk into him from all directions. Sean and the girl's eyes are bright blue. "Who's the chic?", asks Adam. "Her name is White Lightning", says Sean. She of course can not see the Shadow nor the Reaper. "My name's Adam", he says standing at four hundred pounds. "Adam is my brother". "Sorry I knocked you out, I was just protecting my brother". "You are foregiven", she says. Sean turns to her, "Now how about that date?" "Yes. What is a date?", she asks. "I get to treat you to a feast and entertainment", he says. "Oh. In that case then you'll have to follow me". She turns around and starts walking across the field. Sean looks at the Shadow. He moves his arm outward as to say proceed. "Come on Adam!", says Sean. The Shadow stays behind with the Reaper as Sean and Adam follow the girl.

They arrive in a small village not to far away. "We need to stop", says Sean. "What's wrong?", asks Adam. "I don't know. I feel weird" He looks down at his hands. They begin to grow as well as his arms and legs. He now looks like he's on steroids. "Dude! What the hell? You get muscles while I turn into the blob?" "Must be something with the atmosphere", she says. She smiles, because she likes what she sees. "We must continue onward" They keep walking through town as people bow down as they walk by. "Why are they bowing to us?", asks Adam. "They're not bowing to you. They're bowing to me", she says. "Why?" "Because I'm the damn queen that's why". "Your kidding. What exactly are you the queen of?" "I am the queen of this planet" "What is the name of this planet?" "It has no name. The people here decided long ago not to label it. The reasons are unknown". "So where's your king?", asks Sean. She stops walking and turns to him. "He was killed in battle defending his people from the evils of this world and now I'm left to pick up the pieces". She turns and keeps walking. Sean and Adam follow. Adam motions to Sean to keep talking to her. He walks quickly to her side and asks, "So how does one become your king?" "Why do you ask such a question?" Sean grabs her arm and they stop walking. "I want to be your king" She pauses as Sean lets go. "You have proven yourself worthy already", she says. Sean smiles. She starts walking again and says, "Now we just have to work on your tact". Adam walks by Sean and high fives him.

They arrive at the edge of some woods. She stops and turns around. "If you look up you will see my castle up on a mountain. To get there we must go through these woods. In there you will encounter many obsticles such as demons, traps and worst of all the doorway that leads you to the castle. Adam laughs saying, "What's so scary about a door?" She walks up to him. "Laugh now, runaway later". He stops laughing. She turns around and walks up to Sean. "Are you ready?" He looks at Adam and asks, "Are you ready?" Adam nods. She looks at the woods and says, "Let's go then". They walk slowly into the opening of the woods. Adam pulls his sword out, ready for anything that might jump out at him. Adam and the queen hold their arms out to their sides ready to shock. Strange yelling sounds are heared. "Yow!" About five minutes go by when from out of nowhere Adam is attacked by a demon. It tackles him to the ground. Adam wrestles with it while punching it in the head. Even as big as Adam is he doesn't match the strenght of the skinny black demon. The queen shocks the demon while Sean grabs a tree branch. The demon is thrown back. Sean beats the demon with the branch smashing its head in. He then runs over to Adam. "Are you ok?" "I'm fine. That thing was strong". The queen walks up, "Imagine fighting a hundred of them at one time". Sean helps Adam up and dusts him off. "We must keep moving. The demons burnt hair will attract more", the queen says. They continue to walk further into the dark depths of the woods. A sudden stink comes to Sean. "Ew. What's that smell?" Adam gets a wiff as well. "Man you ain't kiddin", he says as he covers his nose. "All I smell is someone cooking a an anal glan of a horned toad", the queen says while breathing in with delite. Sean and Adam tear pieces of clothing to cover their noses. "How can you stand that?", asks Sean. "It is considered to be a traditional food", she says. Chanting is heard from around the corner, but they can't make out what they are saying. "We must be careful. This might be a trap", the queen says. The smell becomes more of a spell to the queen and she begins to fall for it. She runs toward it almost sprinting like. "Wait!", yells Sean. As she rounds the corner, she is confronted by a crowd of demons celebrating. Sean and Adam catch up quickly, but it is too late. The demons stop celebrating and try to attack them. Sean stands beside his queen with arms spread outward. Adam stands behind them. Little electric bolts flow out of their fingertips. The demons prepare to fight. A loud roar is heard from behind. The demons back off and fall on one knee. A larger demon comes flying out from behind them. He stands ten feet tall holding a staff and wearing a cape. On his chest is a gold plate with detailed engravings. Around his waist is a gold skirt. The queen knows who he is and knows he is a demon of great power. She immediately bows to him. "Bow down!", she tells Sean and Adam. They do as well. "Why have you interupted our great ceremony?", the demon asks with an unusual deep voice. "Please forgive us. We are just trying to get to the castle", she says while looking down at the ground. She knows that with her powers and

Sean's that they could destroy all of them, but she doesn't, because she wants to see if she can be allies with the demons. "Rise", says the demon. All three rise to their feet. "If you want to pass you must pass a challenge. The fat one must fight one of my best. If he wins you may pass" The queen looks back at Adam. "Are you up to it?" "Do I have a choice?" "Nope" "Then I guess I except your challenge", he says with sarcasm. "Let the battle begin!", the demon yells. The crowd roars, "Roar!" They make a large circle and Adam steps in as Sean and the queen watch from the side. "So where is this great warrior of yours?", Adam asks. A figure flies over the crowd as they look up. It lands right in the middle of the circle. Its long black wings cover it as it crouches. They open as it stands and fold back. It's a beautiful demon woman with glowing white eyes. Her face has cracks all over and her lips are black. She has long black hair and wears a bikini made out of black jungle root and carries a large staff. Her skin is light grey and full of death. "Wow", thinks Adam. The demon shouts, "Fight!" She lunges at him with her staff. "Yah!" She smacks him on his head breaking the staff. He staggers a bit, but it does little damage. "I don't want to hit a girl", he says. The dark angel runs over to him with extreme speed and knocks him to the ground. "Come on Adam! Get up!", shouts Sean. He climbs to his feet. She tries to hit him, but he catches her fist. "Ah!", she screams. The more he squeezes the more she screams. She falls to her knees. "Ha ha", says Adam. She reaches up and hits him in the balls. "Oh!" He lets go of her as he falls to the ground grabbing himself. She gets up and tries kicking him, but he doesn't feel it over the other pain. "You fat piece of crap!", she shouts. He grabs her leg as she kicks him and she falls backwards. He then rolls over on top of her crushing her chest. A tear runs down her cheek. Adam shows mercy and lets up. Her chest forms back. Adam lays by her side trying to catch his breath. She does the same. "Enough!", the great demon says. "This is no fight. I am not amused. You three may pass and don't ever try to come back through here again". The queen walks up to him and asks, "I would much greatly appreciate it if we could become allies" The demon looks down at her and says, "You must gain my respect first". "How?", she asks. The demon looks onward, "You must make it out of here alive". She backs up and stands with Sean and Adam. Looking at Sean she holds out her hand to him. He grabs it. "You ready for this?", she asks. "Nope", he replies. The wind starts to gather as they raise their arms together. Black clouds form above. Lightning strikes hitting a couple of the demons and knocking them to the ground. The large demon charges Sean and the queen. Lightning hits the demon, but does nothing. Out of nowhere, Adam slams into the demon knocking him to the ground. He stands over top of him. "This fight isn't over", says Adam. Sean and the queen concentrate on the other demons while Adam fights the larger one. Adam is tackled and beaten, but fights back as well. The fallen Angel flies off as demons are shocked to a crisp. Adam gets the large demon in a head lock and breaks his neck. "Crack!" He throws the demon to the ground and backs up. After all of the demons are destroyed, Sean, Adam and the queen are the only ones left standing. "So much for making them our allies", she says. "Shall we continue?", says Sean waving his hand and breathing heavily. He puts his arm around Adam. "Not bad", he tells him. "I'm hungry", Adam replies. They laugh it off and keep walking.

About halfway up, they come to a small cottage. An old man and woman work out in a garden. The queen stops. "This could be a trap", she says. "Are you kidding? It's just a little old lady and man", says Adam. "Yeah. What's the worst that could happen?", asks Sean shrugging his shoulders. They continue walking to the house. "Hello there!", says the old man. "Oh. We have quests!", says the old woman. Sean, Adam and the queen are greeted with smiles. "I bet you folks are hungry? We have plenty to eat as you can see", says the old man. He leads the boys inside as the old woman leads the queen. "You look familiar to me", says the old woman to the queen. "I'm sure we've never met", says the queen. "Do come in and take a load off" As they enter the house the old woman brings up the rear. Just before she closes the door she looks around outside and sniffs the air and slams the door shut. Inside, the old man walks over to a fire place and sees his fire has gone out. "Damn! I let the fire go out again" Sean walks over. "Allow me to help you with that sir" He puts a couple pieces of wood on and holds his hand up. Fire comes out of his fingertips. The old man stands back. Sean touches the wood and lights it. He blows his fingers out and says, "There you go", with a smile. The old man can't believe his eyes. "You mind explaining to me how you did that?" "I got hit by lightning", Sean replies. "Ok. Who's hungry?", the old woman asks. She brings out a plate of sandwiches and sets them on the table. Everyone grabs one and begins eating. "Um. This is good. What is it?", asks Adam. "Goat", she says. "That's not weird at all", replies Sean with sarcasm. "You must eat it all. It will give you great strenght", says the queen. They finish the sandwiches and sit down in the den in front of the fire. "So where is it that you come from?", asks the old man. "We are from here", says the queen, "We are on our way to the castle". "Oh yes. The castle. It holds great powers there. So I've been told", says the old woman. "How is it you two are living in the middle of this demonic forest and haven't been eaten", asks Sean. The old man and woman look at each other and smile. "There are much more worst things in these woods than demons you know", says the old man. "Like what?", asks Adam. "Like people like us", the old woman replies as she laughs. "Ha ha ha!" "Well we must be going now", says the queen as she gets up and heads for the door. The old woman quickly stands between her and the door. "Well you three must stay for desert". Adam gulps, "What's for dessert?" The old woman looks at him and smiles, "You are!" The old man pulls a lever and the whole living room floor opens up. Sean and Adam fall straight down about ten feet and the old woman pushes the queen down below as well. The old man pushes the lever and the floor closes. Adam lands on his face and Sean lands on his back. The queen lands on top of Sean. All three land on a pile of hay. The old man and woman can be heard above laughing. The queen climbs off of Sean and he gets up. He shouts out, "Really? Do you know who you are messing with? We could burn this place down!" One of the walls opens up. "What do you suppose is in there?", asks Adam. The sound of a motor starts up. Adam tries to get a closer look. A giant row of saw blades appear. "Look out!", shouts Sean. Adam dives out of the way. Sean and the queen blow the blades apart with there abilities. "Boom!" The wall shuts and spikes come out from all of the walls. Adam gets up and asks, "Are you thinking what I'm thinking?" "Quick! Get in the middle of the room!", says Sean. The walls start to move as Sean and the queen use their powers to force them back. Sean's strenght increases as vains show. The queen grits her teeth. With their backs touching, the power increases even more. Sean catches both of them on fire. It is something that she has never felt before. Adam covers his eyes as all four walls explode. "Boom!" The top opens as the old man stands with a rifle in his hands. Sean and the queen don't hesitate. They aim at the old man and hit him with supernova. They wait to see if the old woman is going to do anything, but she has vanished. Adam stands up against the wall as Sean climbs up first. The queen climbs up next as Sean pulls her up. "I'm going to go find a ladder", says Sean. The queen waits with Adam. Sean takes off out the front door and around the back. "Your brother is amazing you know. I like him alot" "He's the best. I would die for him". As Sean looks around the back of the house for a ladder he sees a weird weapon leaning up against a shed. It's a huge curved sword on the end of a shaft. "This looks like the one the Reaper uses except bigger", he says to himself. He opens the door to the shed and two dead demon bodies fall out. "I guess they didn't taste very well" As he looks, he see a ladder to his right. He grabs it and backs out of the shed. He looks over to his right at the giant weapon. He decides to take it with him. As he rounds the house, he hears the sounds of demons off in the distant. "They must have smell the bodies", he says. He runs back in the house, puts the weapon down and slides the ladder down in the hole. "We have to move fast. The demons are on their way". Adam climbs out and Sean picks up the weapon. They head out of the house and keep going up the mountain running as fast as they can. As they enter the woods, the old woman comes out of the house with a butcher's knife in hand. She turns to run after them, but just as she does the demons come out of the woods. She looks back and screams, "Ah!" She is too slow. The demons catch up to her and rip her apart. One by one, her limbs are torn from her body with nothing left but the torso. "I thought we killed them all?", asks Adam. The queen looks at him and says, "Where there are some there are many more to kill". She turns and keeps walking. Sean walks behind her as Adam follows. He looks at the weapon that Sean is carrying and asks, "Where'd you find that thing?" "Back behind the house. It might bring us some luck". "Sure is big. You don't think it will slow you down?" "It's actually very lite" "It looks like something you find on a video game", Adam chuckles. They continue their journey up the mountain and through the woods.

The queen stops in her tracks just ahead of Sean and Adam. They catch up to her and stand at her side. "You've got to be kidding me", says Adam. A giant gap stands between them and the otherside with a river at the bottom of it. "Dude, there's no way I'm jumping this", says Adam. Sean holds the giant weapon at his side, while playing with a knob with his thumb on the shaft of it. He accidently pushes the knob and the end of the weapon shoots outward with a chain attached to it and flies across the gap and sticks into the otherside. The queen looks at Sean with big eyes. "I did that on purpose", he says. "Sure you did", she says. She walks over and stands behind him grabbing the shaft. "We need to pull together", she says. "We are not that strong". "It's an illusion. Help us Adam". He walks over and grabs the shaft as well. Adam counts, "One two three". "Ah!" The mountain on the otherside begins to shake and move. It moves so fast that it hits the otherside making them fall. The demons are heard not too far behind. "Roar!" Sean presses the button again and the chain retracts. He pulls the end out of the rock and they start climbing. "I don't know if I can make it Sean", says Adam. "You have to try", says Sean. They let him go first. Incredibly, he climbs with amazing strenght. "It must be the atmosphere", says Sean. "You go now my queen", Sean says as he follows. They get about halfway up when the demons arrive. They waste no time clawing their way up faster than Sean, Adam and the queen. One grabs Seans leg and yanks him off. He goes flying into a crowd of demons. Another demon bites the queens ankle as well and sends her sliding down. Adam looks down, "No!" Almost at the top he looks up. He gets a mean face and pushes off. Four hundred pounds of sumo splash are about to cause a big boom. He lands on the crowd of demons squashing some. The demons back up as he climbs to his feet. Sean and the queen do as well. She looks down and notices she is bleeding from her side. She lifts up her shirt exposing a huge gash caused by one of the demons. The demons smell the blood and it sends them into a frenzy. All of them dive at her, but Sean is there to blow them back with his lightning. One by one, he slings his arms out flinging electricity. The demons keep coming. Sean gets so hot he builds up too much power and catches his body on fire. He brings his arms back and slings them to the front sending a huge wave of fire down the mountain. It burns up everything in sight. The demons turn to ash, but the trees regrow in a matter of seconds. His flame dies out as the queen stands in pain. She falls to the ground. "My queen!", shouts Sean. He kneels at her side. "Give me your hand", she says. "Touch my wound with your heat". Sean heats his hand up and rubs her cut. It smooths over as if she were made out of wax. He then helps her up. "Are you ok?", asks Adam. My wound is, but if I don't get medicine soon I will die. They climb the mountain as she struggles. Adam is the first to reach the top with no problem. Sean follows the queen as she reaches the top as well. Adam helps her up and Sean, too. "Isn't there a better way to get to the castle like a driveway?", asks Adam. "There is, but it is on the otherside of the mountain" "Well. That's just great". They do find a small path to walk along. "This is like some kind of bike trail or something", Seans says. "What's a bike?", she asks. "It's this thing you ride with two wheels", says Adam. "Sounds like fun" She begins to feel nauseous. She stops walking. "Adam can you carry me?" "Yeah" He walks up to her and throws her over his shoulder. As they walk a little further, they encounter what looks like a giant black door. Adam sets her down for a moment and walks up to the door. "I can't find a knob" Sean walks up beside him and stares at it as well. "Have you ever seen such a weird looking door?", he asks. The ground begins to trimble and all three fall to the ground. The door changes shape and turns into a mirror. Adam gets up, as well as the others. He walks back up to the mirror and sees his reflection. He looks back at the queen and asks, "So how do we open this door?" He looks back and his reflection has changed. He now sees his worst fear which is himself, but about weighing about a thousand pounds. "As he screams, he loses his balance and falls backwards. Sean glances into the mirror and sees himkself as a little kid. It startles him and he kicks the mirror. It breaks into tiny pieces and falls to the ground. "Well, that's one way to open it", she says. Sean steps through as the queen follows. She leans down at Adam and whispers, "Told you". Adam picks himself up and follows. They continue walking until they walk out of the woods. "There it is", says Sean. "We might encounter some guards on the way in so keep a look out", he says. As they arrive at the main gate, sure enough two guards yell out, "Halt! "Who are you?" "I am Sean and this is my brother Adam. We come in piece. We also have your queen. She is very sick. She has been scratched by a demon". "Don't move", says one of the guards. The gate opens and four guards come rushing out holding swords. Sean puts his hands up. Adam doesn't move a muscle. The guards get behind them and march them in. A man comes running out. "My queen! What has happened here?"

"She has been scratched by a demon. Her wound is heeled, but she is very sick", says Sean. "Bring her this way", the man says. He turns and walks while they follow. They enter a room filled with beautiful woman and strong looking men. "Lay her down on this bed", he says. Adam gently lays her down and backs away. As Adam walks by the man, the man can't help but say, "My God your fat". Adam pays him no attention. "Let's have a look at you", he says as she moans. "Oh yes. I have just the thing" He runs out of the room for a moment. Sean walks to the otherside of the bed and grabs her hand. He leans over and whispers something in her ear and then leans back. She begins to caugh a little as she breaks out in a fever. The man walks back in with a cup filled with something. "Here we go. Drink this". She takes the cup and gulps it. The man then takes the cup from her as she coughs a little. Within minutes she begins to feel better. "What is that? It stinks", says Adam as he covers his nose. "It's a combination of a couple of dead animals and plants", the man says. Sean leans over to her and says, "Are you feeling better?" "Yes", she says and smiles. A man comes running in the room shouting, "The demons are coming!" "We must get out of here", says Sean. "There is secret door in the back", the man says. Adam helps the queen up as the man leads the way. Sean follows. As they walk into a back room, the man reaches up on a wall and pulls a lit torch. The wall begins to move outward and then slides to the right exposing the woods outside. As the man steps out he is attacked by demons. Adam, the Queen and Sean make a run for it. The demons chase them, but are cut down by Sean's lightning. The Queen stops and turns around. She watches demons cover the castle like a black darkness. Sean runs up to her and grabs her arm, pulling her toward the woods. She turns and runs with him and Adam. They disappear into the night.

About a mile in, they seek camp and build a small fire. Sean sits as the Queen lays in his lap. Adam tends to the fire. "I'm starving", says Adam. The Queen rises up. "I'll go get us something" "Are you going to be ok?", asks Sean. "Don't worry", she says. "These are my woods remember" She smiles and walks away. Minutes go by. Sean and Adam wait patiently. Suddenly, there is a bright white light and a zap coming from the direction that she walked in. Sean and Adam rise to their feet. The Queen walks out from the blackness holding three strange looking rat-like animals. She throws them on the ground. "Dinner is served", she says.

The next morning Sean awakens to find himself lying in a hospital bed. His vision is blurred and he has all kinds of tubes running to him. "Sean?" He looks to his right and sees his mother sitting beside his bed. She smiles. "Am I dreaming?", he asks. "No", she says. "What happened to me mom?" "You've been in a coma for a long time now" His vision begins to clear. He barely recognizes her. "I'll go get the nurse" She gets up from her chair and walks out of the room. As soon as the door closes, the wall in front of his bed turns into a giant television. He sees Adam and the Queen standing in the forest looking around. The Queen cries out, "Sean!" Adam does the same. "Sean!" His mother walks back in the room with the nurse. "Well hello sleepy head", the nurse says with a smile. Sean looks at her then back at the wall. The wall has become just a wall now. "How are you feeling Sean?", asks the nurse. "Ok", he replies. She takes out her small flashlight and looks into his eyes. She then turns the flashlight off and rises up. "Are you hungry?", she asks. "Yes" "I'll be right back" She turns around and walks out of the room. While she is away, Sean's mother walks over to his side and pulls up a chair. She sits down and reaches for Sean's hand. "I'm sorry that this has happened to you Sean. I blame myself everyday for not being there for you and Adam. Maybe if I were a better mother . . . I" She tries to hold back the tears, but can't. "Don't blame yourself for my stupidity mom" Sean suddenly remembers that he saw her die earlier. "Am I dreaming?" "Of course not", she says. "It's just that . . . well . . . I saw you die" "It was just a dream Sean. Everything's ok now" "Where's Adam and dad?" She looks away and tries to hold back the tears again. "Both your father and Adam are missing" She looks back at him. "Did they go looking for me?" "Why would they do that? You've been here the whole time" Sean becomes light headed. His eyes roll back into his head. "Sean!" "Nurse!", she shouts. He passes out.

It is daybreak and Adam and the queen run for their lives through a wheat field. Panting for air, they both try to escape the demons that hunt them. "I see a small house!", she says. "Better not be any old people living there", shouts Adam. They make it to the front door. She reaches for the knob and turns it. She then opens the door quickly. They both duck inside and slam the door behind them. Adam runs up to the window and watches the demons run by. The queen stands in the middle of the room looking around. "I don't think anyone lives here", she says judging by the way the place looks. Adam joins her. "There's a fireplace. I'll start a small fire", he says. "I hope you don't think we are staying in here tonight", she says with a tone. Adam looks at her and says, "Why not? It's shelter" "I have strict morals that's all", she replies. "In my family no man and woman shall sleep in the same room together unless they are married" "Aren't you being a little rediculess? Ok. Let me make it easy for you. Do you have a thing for me?" "Eww. Hell no. I find you discusting" "Well there you have it. I don't like you in that way either" Adam of course was lying, but he'd do anything to get a good nights rest. "Ok then. Since you put it that way I guess it will be alright" "Great!", replies Adam sarcasticly. He makes his way to the door. "By the way, if you can you should get us another rodent to eat. I'm going to go get some wood" He opens the door and walks out slowly.

Sean opens his eyes to find himself lying on the floor face down in what appears to be a pool of blood. The whole right side of his face is covered. He raises up and wipes it away quickly saying, "Gross". As he looks around the room he asks, "where the hell am I now?" He turns and looks behind him to find an old, large, dusty mirror on the wall. He walks up to it and wipes away the dust with the sleeve from his arm. His eyes grow large as the reflection shocks him. The person in the mirror is not him, but rather the Reaper. "No!", he shouts, breaking the mirror with his fist. As he backs up, the mirror explodes into a thousand pieces. He covers his face and turns away. As he turns around, he sees another body lying in the pool of blood face down with half its head missing and a shotgun beside it. Sean leans over and turns the body over. "No!", he shouts as he begins to cry. "Dad?" He recognizes him right away. Aparently, when Sean saw his old dad that day at the cabin it trigered something in his dad right after he told him to leave. Sean now realizes where he is as he runs out the front door. He stops right at the bottom of the steps and looks around. He then runs around to the back of the cabin where he finds his dad's car. "I hope the keys are in it", he thinks to himself. He runs around to the driver's side and opens the door. The keys aren't in the ignition so he looks on top of the sunvisor. Nothing is there either. He then reaches over and opens the glovebox. An old revolver presents itself. Sean pauses, but then grabs the pistol and checks to see if it's loaded. Sure enough the gun is loaded completely. He then lays it on the seat beside him and wonders where the keys are. He then sees in front of him a small ash tray. He reaches down and opens it. He pulls out a single key and sticks it in the ignition. He closes his eyes and says, "please start". He turns the key and the car starts right up. "Yes!" He puts it in drive and takes off down the driveway.

Out on the main road, Sean listens to the radio. Every station he turns it to is the same. A man says, "Attention! Please stay inside and lock your doors. An outbreak of gigantic porportions has hit the planet. Right now there is no cure. Please use extreme caution if you must go outside. The dead have risen" Sean's first thought is his father. He believes he knows now what happened to his father. He drives all night not knowing where he is going. All he does is head east praying that he might find someone that isn't affected. He pulls off to rest at an old gas station. He turns the car off and looks around to see if it's safe to get out. No one appears to be around, but the light are on inside the building. He grabs the pistol and puts it in his pants. He then opens the door and gets out while looking around. He slowly walks up to the door of the place, opens it and enters. The door chimes as country music plays in the back ground. A man comes out of the back room wiping his hands with a rag. "Can I help you?" This startles Sean making him pull his pistol. The man ducks saying, "just take the money! I just work here!" Sean puts the pistol away and says, "sorry. You startled me. I don't want to rob you" The man rises up slowly. "Damit boy. You almost gave me a heart attack" "Sorry. Have you heard about the outbreak?" "Sure have. It's all over the radio. Been listening to it all day" "Why are you still here? Should'nt you be where it's safe?" "Trust me. It's safe here. Come in the back and I'll show you" Sean follows the man to the back room. They stop before the man opens the door. "Wait till you see this", he says with a smile. He opens the door and the room is filled with a multitude of guns and ammo. "Holy crap! You got a lot of guns" "I know", the man giggles. Sean walks around checking out the guns while the man walks on the other side. "My name's walt. People say I'm a little crazy, but I bet I got more guns than they do. While they're out there getting that outbreak shit I'm in here where it's safe. You gotta name? "Sean" "Nice to meet you Sean. You can trust me. I'm the good guy. I'm usually the one that gets picked on or chosen last, but I always come out in the end laughin. Say, that's a nice revolver you got there" "It was my dad's" "Most sons get guns from their dads. My gave me all these. He was in the war" "You got anything to eat walt?" "Sure do. Come on out. I'll fix you something" Walt walks out of the room followed by Sean. "How come you being so nice to me?" "Well, you're probably going to be the last human I come face to face with so why not? Besides, I'm not going to be running this buisness anymore so we might as well take advantage of what it has to offer.

Like little kids, they both run up and down the isles grabbing everything they can. Soon they find themselves sitting behind the counter eating it all. Before they know it, they've eaten too much. "Ah. I can't eat anymore", says Sean. "Me neither", says Walt rubbing his belly. He lays back and lights up a cigarette while looking at a magazine. "What is such a big deal about celebrities?", he asks. "I mean they're people just like us. They get out of bed just like us. They put on pants just like us. Hell they even take a shit just like us" Sean giggles. "I mean what is the big deal?" "I don't get it either. If you ask me there should be a law against shit like that", he says pointing to the magazine. "I tell you what would be cool. After all of this outbreak ends they should have a magazine showing which celebs are zombies now. Then I would buy one" They both laugh histericly. "You know what I like to read? Comic books", says Walt as he reaches up and grabs one off the counter. "Why comics?" "Because, with comics I can get carried away with imagination. You know it's not real, but you sometimes wish you could be a superhero and have special powers" "What kind of powers would you have Walt?" "I would be able to shoot lightning from my fists and fly of course. What about you?" Sean shrugs his shoulders and laughs a little. Walt laughs along with him.

As they finish laughing, someone bangs on the front door. Walt looks at Sean with a blank face. The banging continues. They both raise up slowly and peek over the counter. "What they hell is that?", asks Walt. "Zombie", says Sean. Walt grabs his gun. "No wait. As long as they can't get in we're safe" Walt lowers is gun. More zombies appear out of nowhere and walk slowly up to the door. "Is there a way to the roof?", asks Sean. "Yeah. Follow me" Walt turns around and walks quickly through the back. He walks up to a ladder made onto the far wall and climbs it while holding a rifle. On the roof, a lid opens and they climb out. Walt runs over to the front ledge and looks down. Sean follows. "How many do you see?", asks Sean. "About twenty" "What do you think we should do?" "Try blowing their heads off I guess" Sean prepares himself for what he's about to tell Walt. "I've got a better idea Walt. There's something I haven't told you about me. I have a super power. I can shoot lightning out of my fists" Walt gets discusted and says, "Damn it. That was my idea" "I'm serious Walt" "Yeah ok. I'll go get more guns and ammo", he says as he turns to go back down stairs. With his back towards Sean, Sean brings his arms up to his sides and begins to produce electricity. Walt stops and turns around. "Holy crap! How are you doing that?" Sean turns around and jumps off the roof and into the crowd of zombies. He grabs two of them as they shake and their heads blow off. Sean catches on fire as well as all the other zombies. Walt can only stare and smile. Sean gets so heated that his flame turns blue and the zombies turn to fine ash.

When the dust clears Sean is left standing, looking up at Walt. Walt, standing in shock turns around and runs back over to the roof door and climbs down the ladder. He runs to the front door with rifle in hand and stops just before it. He opens it slowly and walks through the ash looking down and all around. "How did you do that?", he asks. "I was hit by lightning", replies Sean. "Man. I need to get hit by lightning" Sean giggles a little. "It's a little more complicated than that. Sean turns around to see more zombies slowly headed his way. "Walt, you need to get back inside" As Sean turns back around, a zombie comes from behind Walt and attacks him. Walt yells out in pain, "Ahh!" The zombie tears through his arm like a meat grinder. Sean runs up to it and kicks it away. The zombie flies through the front window of the store. Walt falls to his knees. "Walt are you ok?" With his head hung over, Walt struggles to stay contious. Sean

97

walks slowly over to him and asks again, "Are you ok?" Walt doesn't respond. Sean reaches down to shake him, but as he does Walt looks up slowly. His eyes are white and his skin has turned greyish blue. He lets out a moan, "Mmmm" Sean backs up, while Walt rises to his feet and reaches out for him. "Oh no Walt. Not you, too" Not looking where he's going, Sean backs up into the zombie that he kicked through the window. He falls to the ground and rolls over on his back. As he's looking up, Walt and the zombie crowd over top of him as if to eat him. Sean can only do one thing. He closes his eyes and catches himself on fire.

He raises up quickly in bed with sweat running down his face and breathing fast. He looks around the almost dark room with just enough light shinning through a window. Rain trickles down the window and thunder is heard off in the distance. His heart monitor is fast at first, but begins to slow down. He looks around the room slowly and comes across a figure sitting in the corner to his right. "Mom?" The figure leans forward to where the light hits its face. "Hello Sean. How are you feeling?" "The Reaper!", says Sean. The Reaper stands in human form. "I feel good", says Sean. "Liar!", shouts the Reaper. Lightning flicker as thunder follows. The Reaper smiles saying, "Can you feel it Sean? Can you feel it corsing through your vains?" With each flicker Sean's thurst grows. The Reaper laughs, "Mmwahaha!" "Am I dreaming?", Sean asks. "Let's find out", says the Reaper. He lifts his arms and Sean rises out of bed and floats over to his right and lands on his feet. The Reaper then waves his hand and the heartbeat monitor line comes off. The sound of flatline is heard. Sean walks over to the Reaper in front of the bed. He looks back and sees his body still lying in bed. Two nurses come rushing in. One of them tries giving Sean c.p.r., but it is useless. Sean looks back at the Reaper and asks, "So where are you taking me now?" The Reaper morphs back into his original body. He then turns to his right and waves his right hand opening a portal. In the portal, Sean can see his father, mother and brother waiting on the other side. His brother waves for him to come through, but Sean notices something weird. His eyes flash a red glow for a split second. "What the hell is this?" The Reaper shoves him in and what he thought was his family has now become a room full of unwanted souls. Sean struggles to get through an endless crowd. He cries out in agony, "Help me! God please help me!" He tries to use his power, but it doesn't work. As he falls to the ground he is trampled. Even though he can't die he still feels pain. He closes his eyes and wishes for all to go away. About a hundred feet away, bodies begin to fly left and right as something bulldozes through them. Sean opens his eyes and tries to stand. He can barely make out the figure as it smacks people out of the way and gets closer and closer. It finally reaches Sean as it brings a smile to his face. "It took me awhile, but I found you brother", says Adam. Sean hugs him and thanks him. "How did you know I was here?" "The Reaper lead me here" "Mom and dad . . . they're dead" "I know. They're here, too. Now we must find them. I brought a little help with me" Adam moves to his side. "Hello Sean" Sean falls to his knees and bows his head. "My queen. I thought I'd never see you again" "You may rise Sean" He stands slowly. "Where are we?", he asks. "Hell I think", she replies. "Your brother and I have been traveling so long. We were both captured and tortured to death by demons. Even with my powers we could not escape. They were too stronge" Adam speaks, Apparently our souls came here to hell. For what reason, we don't know" "Atleast we're together", says Sean. Adam puts his left hand on Sean's right shoulder and asks, "Do you still have your powers?" "No. I need a recharge I think" "Well, let's get out of here", says Adam. They turn and walk through the crowd of people. One man staggers into Adam. Adam pushes him into others knocking them down like bowling pins. As they walk off into the darkness, the crowd closes back up like the sea.

Back at what use to be Sean's house, their mother fights off demons trying to harm her. She holds a stick and is backed into a corner. When the house caved in on her she was sent into a parallel universe of hell. A dozen or so demons surround her. If they get their hands on her she will be ripped apart over and over. She franticly tries to run out of the house, but ends up falling. The demons pounce on her. She fights them and stabs one of them in the eye. Yelling and crying, she crawls out of the house. She kicks the demons off one by one. As she crawls down the front steps bloody and bashed the demons start to back off. The farther away she gets from the house the less the demons chase. She makes it to the front lawn and turns over on her back proping herself up with her arms. The demons stand in her crushed house snarling and staring at her. "They must have a boundary", she says to herself. She gets up off the ground saying, "Ha! As long as I'm out here you can't touch me!" She looks to her right and sees her neighbor standing on the front steps waving for her to come over. The old woman smiles with green teeth, "come on over deary" Connie doesn't hesitate. She runs right over without knowing what her neighbor is. "Thank God! Those things were trying to kill me" "God had nothing to do with that", the old woman says. "Come inside where it's safe" Connie walks past the woman and into the house. The woman looks back at the demons and knods her head. The demons knod back. She follows Connie into the house and slams the door behind her. Seconds later a scream is heard from inside.

As Sean, Adam and the queen walk they can barely see through the darkness. They walk side by side ready to face their next challenge. A bright white light presents itself in front of them. "Do not be afraid", a voice says. They stop walking and the queen asks, "Who are you?" "I am the gate keeper" "Gate for what?", asks Adam. "The gate to Heaven" They look around trying to find someone, but all they hear is the voice. "We would like to pass, but we are looking for two people. Could you help us?" "Perhaps, but is your faith strong?" "Yes", replies Sean. "We are looking for my mother and father" "Oh, yes. I know of the ones that you speak" "Well, where are they?", asks Sean. "They are in the same place in which they died" Sean looks back at Adam and the queen, "What does that mean?" The voice speaks, "It means when they died they entered a parallel universe known as Hell. Your mother should still be at your house and your father should still be at the cabin" The queen steps forward, "What happens if we find them? Can we all go to Heaven?" The voice pauses and then answers, "Yes" "Great! So how do we get out of this place?", asks Sean. "Usually, we are not allowed to help, but your faith seems stronger than most" From out of the white light an angel walks out dressed in armor and long white wings. "This is our warrior angel. He will help track your mother and father" "Does he have a name?", asks the queen with lust in her eyes. "I have no name", he responds. "Ok. Lets go", says Adam as he turns around and starts walking away. The warrior doesn't move. "Well, you coming or not?", asks Sean. "There's a quicker way", says the warrior. He turns to his right and waves his hand. A large portal opens. "Shall we", he says motioning to the portal. The queen walks through as everyone else follows. On the other side they appear outside of their dad's cabin. Guns shots ring out. They take cover as the warrior steps out and looks around. A bullet grazes his armor. "Get down!", Sean shouts. "Nothing can hurt me", the warrior says. The portal closes as the warrior steps away. Inside the house, their dad fires off round after round at demons trying to get him. The warrior runs up to the front door as Adam follows. The warrior rips the door down and walks inside. The queen and Sean follow Adam. Their dad is soon out of bullets, but just as the demons get to him the warrior knocks them out of the way. Their dad stands with his arms up in front of him. "Dad!", yells Adam. The warrior stands out of the way. Sean runs in and him and Adam hug their dad. "I thought I'd never see you guys again. Who is this guy and girl?" Sean speaks, "Dad this is a warrior angel from Heaven and the girl is a queen" "Huh?" "Nevermind. We need to get you out of here and find mom" They help him outside and down the steps. "I don't know what the hell is going on and I don't know how much more I can take" "We'll explain later dad. Right now you have to trust us" The warrior waves his hand and another portal opens. "What is that thing?", their dad asks. "It's a time portal. It will take us to your wife", says the warrior. All of them step in as the warrior is the last to enter. Just before he turns to step in a hand grabs his left shoulder and turns him around. The Grim Reaper stands in his original form holding his sythe. It opens his robe and the Shadow steps out. The warrior turns around and closes the portal without going in. He turns back around to face the Shadow. "Hello brother", the Shadow says. "Been a long time Shadow" "They don't belong in Heaven you know" "Says who?" "Says the balance. No soul shall pass into the great Heaven unless he proves himself worthy as a human and neither one of them have done so. So why are you helping them?" "They have proven good faith by showing how much they care for one another so far. You surely are not trying to interfer with that are you Shadow?" "They are not human anymore. Therefore they belong in Hell" "The only thing that belongs in Hell is you!" The warrior whips out his giant sword and tries slicing through the Shadow. The Shadow turns to a cloud of smoke and the sword ends up missing. The Shadow reapears in solid form. "Don't you know that is useless", he says. The

Reaper stands back. "We can't hurt each other so why try?" "It is my duty to protect them. So don't get in my way" "Fine then. I'll make you a deal brother. I won't get in your way as long as you stay out of mine. If I get to them before you do then their souls are mine. Do we have a deal?" "Yes" "Fine then. See you in the next hundred years . . . brother" The Shadow turns around and walks into the Reaper's robe. The Reaper turns to its side and opens a portal. Just before it steps in it looks back at the warrior. It then turns and glides into the portal as it shuts behind it. The warrior takes a deep breath and opens another portal. He steps in and it closes behind him. The portal reopens in front of Connie's house with Sean, adam, their dad and the queen standing on the front lawn. "Why are we here?", asks their dad. "There's nothing here. Your mother died in a car wreck far from here" Sean turns to him and says, "Actually dad, mom died here before the wreck because of some wierd sphere that appeared out of nowhere and destroyed the house. The house crushed her. I think it was my fault, because the sphere was following me" The warrior walks up to Sean and asks, "Was the sphere bright and blue?" "Yeah" "That was an energy ball produced by evil. It was sent out to remove your special power" "Why did it make me strong?", asks the queen. "Possibly, because you are not of this world" Sean walks up to the front steps and sits down. "So if mom died here then where is she?" The warrior looks around. "That is a good question" He looks over and sees the old woman sitting on the front porch in a rocking chair. "Let's ask her?", he says as he starts to walk over. "Be careful. I think she's a demon", Sean says. "Excuse me miss. My friends and I were wondering if you know where we might find the young lady next door?" "Why of course deary. She's inside my house", she says with her rotten smile. "May we come inside?" "Of course" She gets out of the chair and walks over to the door. Just as she reaches for the knob a couple of bugs fall out of her shirt. She turns the knob and everyone is sucked in. A black hole presents itself as everyone except the old woman is sucked through it and spit out the other side. They all land on the ground in a strange world. "Where are we now?", the queen asks. The warrior picks himself off the ground. "It appears that old woman is a gate keeper, too. I must tell the others about her. She may come in handy" "Sean? Adam?" "Mom!" Their mom lay on the ground just a few feet away badly beaten and brused. They rush up to her and hug her. "Mom are you ok?", asks Sean. "I'm ok. Is that you father?" "Hello dear. We've come to rescue you" He reaches down and picks her up in his arms. She breaks down. "Shh. There now. You're safe with us" The warrior walks up. "We can go now if you're ready. There's only one thing. She can not come" "But we came all this way", Adam says. "Not her. Her", the warrior says pointing to the queen. "But why?" "She is not human. She is part of a dream" "What do you mean dream?", Adam asks. "Ask your brother. She is just someone his contious made up" Sean walks over to her. "I'm sorry" "Don't be. Because of you I am real. Even if it is for a little while" She leans over and kisses him on his lips. Sean closes his eyes. She turns to a bright light and disappears. "We must go now", says the warrior. He turns and opens a portal. This time the light is so bright it blinds. He turns and says, "This portal will take you to the front gates" Their father walks up to the portal first carrying his wife. With the children following, they all walk through in single file. When they are all through, the warrior stops and turns around to see if anyone else is following. He smiles a little, turns and walks through as the portal closes behind him.

On the otherside, they all walk out clean and neatly dressed. Instead of carrying Connie, she walks beside her husband without a scratch. Adam follows, slim and a bit muscular with a hair cut. Sean steps through with a big smile on his face and neatly dressed as well. The warrior is the last to step through with his bright shinny armor and sword. A man appears in front of them wearing a long white robe. "Welcome everyone. Sean will you please step forward" Sean walks passed his family and up to the man. "Humans are born into sin. You must prove your faith in order to get into Heaven. You have done so. To risk your life for another is what you have achieved. Your love for your family is great. Adam please step forward" He walks up to the man and stands beside his brother. "You have done so as well. Will the father step forward?" He walks up and stands beside of Adam. "Before you say anything, I would like to say something" The man knods his head. "I know what I did is not exceptable, but I did it because I felt I had nothing else to live for and I didn't want to become a zombie. My family was dead and to live through that . . . well . . . I'd like to see someone try. My family was all that ever meant anything to me" His wife walks up and hugs him as well as his to sons. The man speaks, "What you did was not exceptable, but since your family came for you and they show how much they care for you I will let you pass" The gates open up. "Welcome to Heaven. You may all pass", the man says waving his arm. All four walk past the man smiling and thanking him. As they disappear through the mist the man looks back at the warrior. "Well you've done yet another good deed. How do you feel?" The warrior struts past him saying, "All warrior and no play makes me a dangerous angel"

# ABOUT THE AUTHOR

Since I was a teenager in High School I loved to write poetry. Eventually, it evolved into something more and so I came up with this story. My father has struggled over the years with Diabetes and I know plenty of other people that have been down that road as well. I decided to write a fiction novel based on the Diabetes, but also deal with everyday subjects such as broken families, drugs, alcholism and of there's of cousre the science-fiction of the story which envolves the ever popular outer body experience. When one young man finds out the hard way about Diabetes he falls into a deep coma and the whole time you're stuck wondering if it's all real or not. I also wrote this book to teach the dangers of Diabetes in hopes that the reader will understand, but at the same time be a little on the weird side and add all the impossible things that this story has to offer.

I've lived just about all my life in the little town of Pleasant Garden in North Carolina. It's always been home for me, but I'm the kind of person that can adjust to his enviroment. I consider myself to be very intelligent. I have all kinds of skills and I'm capable of learning just about anything. No one in my family knows where I get it from. I tell them God gave it to me. Without him I am nothing. I truely believe that there is a good reason he gave me the power to write this book even though I hate to read and failed English. I'm very confident in my work that I hope that one day someone will realize it and make it into three movies. I know that there is a lot of competition out there, but there is one thing I have that they don't and that's my book.